Praise for **Yo**
by Jonathar

"*Meres' strong, irreverent characterisation and sharp humour (he was a stand-up comedian) make this a book that will achieve an effortless following.*"
Publishing News

"*With a confidence that announces his inner youth is still alive and slouching, Meres effortlessly reproduces the era of obsession, anxiety and self-consciousness. This is a funny, witty and energetic book for teenagers of all ages.*" Scotland on Sunday

Praise for **Yo! Diary! 2 – And Another Thing . . .**
by Jonathan Meres

"*If you're hooked on Friends, Jonathan Meres' Yo! Diary! 2 is a must. Six teenagers in their individual styles spill their deepest secrets about themselves and reveal their views of each other. And we discover that we're not alone, that others have the same shames and fears and minor joys as we do.*" The Guardian

"*Another year at Molton Secondary sees the usual chaos and hilarity with all the favourite characters in another effervescent diary novel.*" Books magazine

Praise for **Yo! Diary! 2 – And Another Thing . . .**
by Jonathan Meres

Once upon a time, Johnny (Jonathan to his biological parents) Meres was a merchant seaman and an ice-cream man. More recently, as a stand-up comedian, he has won the *Time Out* Award For Comedy and been nominated for The Perrier Award. He has written for and appeared on many radio and TV programmes, including his own series for BBC Radio 4. He lives in Edinburgh with his wife, three sons and no cats. He was once fifteen.

Also available in this series, from Piccadilly Press:
Yo! Diary!
Yo! Diary! 2 – And Another Thing . . .

YO! dOT UK

jonathan meres

Piccadilly Press • London

To Caroline and Alison
– something for the journey . . .

First published in Great Britain in 2001
by Piccadilly Press Ltd.,
5 Castle Road, London NW1 8PR

Text copyright © Jonathan Meres, 2001

Phototypeset from author's disc in 11/18.5 pt Chianti

A catalogue record for this book is available
from the British Library

ISBNs: 1 85340 673 2 (trade paperback)
1 85340 678 3 (hardback)

1 3 5 7 9 10 8 6 4 2

Printed and bound in Great Britain by Bookmarque Ltd.

Design by Judith Robertson
Cover design by Paul Fielding Design Ltd.

JULY

Mandy • JULY 12th

Flipping flip flip. Didn't want to be on stupid 'Rearranging Rooms' anyway, did I? What was I thinking? No, I'm much better off staying in Molton Sodbury for the rest of my life and working at Safebury's in complete obscurity. Well, why not? The career prospects are excellent. So, I might only be on the checkout at the moment, but my boss says that if I'm good he might even let me work on the deli counter some day! Yeah, I know. Whoopy-flipping-do!! Never wanted to be famous anyway. Fame is so totally fickle. As for this whole cult of celebrity thing? Cult of complete pants basically. Bunch of saddos the lot of them, if you ask me. Still haven't heard whether I've got the biscuit commercial, by the way.

Meera • JULY 13th

Poor old Mandy's just about as low as I've ever seen her. This whole 'Rearranging Rooms' thing seems to have really knocked the stuffing out of her. I'm not surprised, mind you. There she was, one minute thinking she was going to be the star of the show and the next thing she knew her bit had been cut out altogether. Now she's all doom and gloom and talking about being stuck in Molton forever. She'll get over it though. At least she hasn't been publicly humiliated by her father and her so-called boyfriend DJ-ing at any discos lately. Ohmygodohmygodohmygod! I'm burning up just thinking about it. Got to go now. There's this fab new Leo De Janeiro website I've just <u>got</u> to check out.

Seb • JULY 14th

Yo! Diary! Check this out, man! Was trying to call Meera all last night but I couldn't get through, which was well frustrating basically. Think she must have been talking to Mandy. Personally I don't know what they find to talk about. I mean, they see each other practically all day every day and then the first thing they do when they get back home is phone each other up! Yeah and when they're not doing that they're texting each other in this well weird language all of their own, dude!

What's wrong with, you know, keeping it real and communicating with a fellow human being on a one to one, eyeball to eyeball basis? Actually, I really should get in touch with Meera. See what's happening. See if she wants to chill or whatever. See if we're still, you know, together basically, man. I'll try and call her again. Yeah, once I've e-mailed my mum to say that I'll be a bit late coming down for tea.

Clare • JULY 15th

Just got sent a load of blurb about the opening of the all-new-revamped-refurbished-re-everythinged community centre. You know, the one designed to keep the likes of me and all the other delinquent scumbags off the streets of Molton Sodbury for the summer. Honestly, you'd think this place was East Central Los Angeles, not just some funny wee town with a pet food factory and a bowling green! Let's face it, the biggest threat to society here is the possibility of bumping into Seb and have him spout garbage at you for three hours. Oh, I'm sure it'll be great. Apparently there's going to be a cybercafé and everything. It's just that I've already got plans for the summer. Not that we're going away or anything, worst luck. Aye well, Mum's only gone and enrolled for some stupid summer school, hasn't she? But hopefully that should be more than compensated for by all the walks in the park and trips to the cinema with Troy. Who knows, there might even be some kissing involved along the way! And then we've got my wee cousin Abi coming down to stay with us for a while. So, all in all, I don't exactly see me spending much time at this community centre, however fantastic and brilliant it's cracked up to be. I can only think that whoever sent me the blurb confused me with someone <u>without</u> a life.

Steven • JULY 16th

Good day 2day. Got sent stuff about community centre. Cybercafé looks gr8. Loads of PCs & everything. Will defin8ly go. 1der who sent it? Very nice of them. Don't get many letters. 1der if I should write back?

Craig • JULY 17th

Think I'm going to have to try and get a job or something for the summer. I don't care what it is. Road sweeper? Chat show host? Astronaut? Anything will do. Just as long as it gets me out of the house from time to time. Just as long as it gets me away from the Incredible Bulk. Or to give her her correct name, Mum. Seems like she's been, you know, thingy forever. It's so humiliating.

Unless, of course, her and Dad have just been winding me up and she's been walking around with a cushion stuffed under her jumper for the last few months. But then why would she want to wind me up? Why pretend that she was having a baby if she's not? Unless, of course, it was just to make me feel even worse than I already do about never having, you know, <u>done it</u>. Mind you, it's going a bit far, isn't it, decorating the box room and turning it into a nursery like that? As for Dad, doing all these stupid breathing exercises? No, she's having a baby all right. So the sooner I get a job the better, I reckon. And as it doesn't look like Steven and I are going to become dotcom millionaires from List.com after all, I suppose I'd better get a copy of the *Molton Times* and start looking under 'Situations Vacant'.

Mandy • JULY 18th

Served Craig in Safebury's today. Boy, is he messed up about his mum being pregnant or what? He went on and on and on about it. It was hysterical. Not that I laughed, of course, because I don't think he actually meant it to be funny. But honestly, all this stuff about his mum with a cushion shoved up her jumper and his dad doing all these breathing exercises and that. What an absolute hoot! And it wasn't just me either. The other customers in the queue obviously thought so too. And the thing is, I only asked him if he'd got a loyalty card! Why Craig never seems to have a girlfriend I have no idea. I mean let's face it, a good sense of humour is the first thing us girls look for in a guy, isn't it? Well, after drop-dead gorgeous looks, a nice six-pack and a pert little backside it's the first thing we look for! Oh, and talking about girlfriend, I think I'll call Meera. That's if I can get through of course. She's been constantly engaged for the past few nights. Maybe I'll text her instead.

Meera • JULY 18th

Why can't Seb be more like Leo? That's what I'd like to know. I don't mean why can't Seb be a big glamorous film star, earn vast amounts of money and pal around with Brad Pittstop like Leo does. What am I? Some kind of reality virgin? And I don't mean why can't Seb look like Leo either. Because let's face it, compared to Leo De Janeiro, anyone's going to look like the back of a bus, aren't they? Ohmygodohmygod, what exactly am I trying to say here? I just wish that Seb was a bit more like Leo in other ways, that's all. Just seeing him in all the magazines and browsing all the websites makes me realise Leo's just . . . well, perfect really. And that Seb just . . . well, isn't really! Oh hang on. Just got a text message from Mandy. What does that one mean again? BT2CU4DHUEOW? Been Told To See You For Dinner Have You Eaten On Wednesday? That can't be right. Doesn't make any sense. Oh, wait a minute. That's it. Been Trying To Call You For Days Have You Emigrated Or What? Oops! Maybe it's time to cut down on the Leo surfing!

Seb • JULY 19th

Community centre? They're having a laugh, man! What would I be doing going to a community centre for Seb's sake! Next thing you know I'll be joining the Scouts and learning to crochet! Not that I'm dissing anyone who does crocheting, by the way. Big up the Crochet Massive, you know what I'm saying? Big up my Gran basically. Respect due! But I mean, come on! Community centres are like death by tedium. They're so last century. Even last century they were so last century, man. We're talking ping-pong. We're talking home-baking. We're talking line dancing. We're talking beards and sandals. We're talking my parents, basically, dude. No, I've got way more important matters to attend to, man. Like mashing up yet more totally hard core sonic mayhem on my trusty decks for a start! Yo!

Molton! Make some noooise!! Altogether now! I'm Slim Madely. Yes, I'm the real Madely, all the other Slim Madelys are just imitators!!

Clare • JULY 20th

Was supposed to be going to see a film with Troy today, but things didn't quite work out as planned. I waited outside the cinema like we'd arranged. Or at least like I thought we'd arranged. Waited for ages, but he never showed up. So I called him on his mobile. He said he was really sorry, but that he was in the hospital visiting his grandma. Touch wood, I've not had to go to the hospital here in Molton yet, but I tell you what, I wouldn't mind. Aye, well it sounds dead trendy and sophisticated. I'm sure I heard someone in the background ordering two cappuccinos and a croissant. Oh well, there's always next time I suppose. Pity though. I was up for a bit of mutual tonsil hoovering. Who knows, we might even have got to see a bit of the film as well!

Steven • JULY 20th

Went in2 town 2day. Wish I hadn't. Was walking past Starbrights. Looked in window. Saw Troy having coffee with girl. Girl not Clare. Maybe from Strange Hill High?

Troy kissed not-Clare girl. Then saw me. Came outside. Acted like me + him R best mates. Asked me not 2 say anything. H8 this kind of thing.

Craig • JULY 21st

Bumped into Steven Stevens in town today. He told me that he knew something but that he couldn't say what it was, which I thought was a bit weird for a start. I mean, that's a bit like saying you've got a present for someone, but that you're not going to give it to them. Well, a bit like that. OK, so it's not like that at all, but anyway that's what he said. So I suggested that he phone me up to tell me instead, but he said no, he couldn't do that because he'd still be saying it wouldn't he? Anyway, to cut a long story short, we decided that Steven should go home and e-mail me and that way he wouldn't actually be <u>saying</u> what he'd got to say, if you see what I mean. So, that's what he did. And I could see straight away why he didn't want to say it. Poor old Clare, eh? I always knew there was something dodgy about Troy. Nobody's that perfect. And with a girl from Strange Hill too! Don't get me wrong, I'm all for being broad-minded and breaking down barriers and prejudices and stuff but, I mean, come on! Not with someone from Strange Hill for goodness sake! Well, I say Clare should dump him. It would serve him right. Not that it's any of our business of course. I was just saying the same thing to Mandy as a matter of fact. And she agreed with me. It's none of our business at all.

Mandy • JULY 21st

Whoa! Hot Goss Central or what? Not exactly earth-shatteringly surprising mind you, since Troy has previously attempted to carry out emergency tonsil-lectomies on both me <u>and</u> Meera! But still! With a girl from Strange Hill too? Now <u>that's</u> juicy! Not only that, but we were treated to another hysterical performance from Craig at the checkout. At this rate, people are going to start deliberately queuing up behind him! He definitely doesn't realise that he's doing it though. But I tell you what, I've seen so-called comedians on the telly who aren't nearly as funny as Craig. It's the way he tells it. All that stuff about Steven not being able to say, so he e-mails him instead! Honestly what a scream. When he finished the whole queue burst into applause. Well, I say 'whole' queue. Only one person didn't join in. The person at the back who we didn't see. Yeah, Clare. Oops.

Meera • JULY 21st

Just got a text from Mandy. The only trouble was I had to phone her up and ask her what the hell it meant! Which kind of defeated the object. Yeah well, how was I supposed to know that TSS4BBNWC stood for Troy Spotted Snogging For Britain But Not With Clare?! What am I, psychic or something? I mean, it could have meant anything, couldn't it? It could have meant Toasted Sausage Sandwiches For Big Bouncing Norwegian With Children for all I know! Aw, poor Clare though. It's really tough when that happens. And I hate to say I told her so, but I told her so. Actually thinking about it, I never did tell her so. But I should have done. Let's face it, those two weren't exactly compatible in the first place, were they, what with Clare being a Taurus and Troy being . . . well, a complete slimeball basically. Not like Leo De Janeiro of course. Leo would never have done anything like that.

Seb • JULY 22nd

OK so the community centre's been like totally done up and there's apparently going to be this amazing new cybercafé or whatever. Two words: <u>so what</u> basically, man? Like this affects me how? Because check this, right? Cybercafés are strictly for the nerds, you know what I'm saying? They're for boffins with no lives or social skills whatsoever. Not that I'm dissing boffins or anything. Yo! Big up boffins. Respect due basically. What I'm trying to say is cybercafés? – *nein danke*, dude! Don't care how state of the art and cutting edge and now and happening they might be. The day that I, DJ Sebsonic, The Groovemaster General am spotted in one of those places is the day when I'll be putting on extra warm socks and thermals. Why? Because hell will have officially just frozen over, dude! And anyway, man, I'm supposed to be going on holiday to Devon with my mum and dad for two weeks in August. Er, I mean Dennis and Marjorie obviously. But I mean that's not something I can get out of at such short notice. And besides, man, it's supposed to be a well wicked caravan site, you know what I'm saying? For real. Seb out.

Clare • JULY 23rd

I am <u>so</u> over Troy it's not true. The guy clearly didn't mean that much to me in the first place. Oh, sure I was upset at the time. But time is a great healer, as they say. OK, so we're only talking three days here, but already I feel so much better about it all. I feel like I've really grown. Really moved on. Like I've learnt from the whole experience. Aye, and the first thing I've learnt is what a complete scumbag Troy is! Honestly, the nerve of the guy! How dare he do that to me? In public too! I mean it's one thing messing around behind my back, but to not even try and be discreet about it! To have his tongue rammed down her throat like that in broad daylight! In the middle of Starbrights! Not caring who saw him! I don't blame her by the way. I'm sure she's very nice. What am I saying? She's clearly a complete tart! And she's from Strange Hill! But like I say, I am so over it now. Time to file and exit. Create a new document. Troy, you are the weakest link. Goodbye!

Mandy • JULY 23rd

Call me cynical, but if Clare really is so over Troy then why can't she stop talking about just how over Troy she is? She called today, apparently to chat about the community centre and how she'd been thinking that it was maybe quite a good idea after all and how she wanted to get dead involved and all that. But actually she spent the best part of an hour and a half telling me how she'd moved on and blah blah blah and how not bothered she was about the whole Troy thing! Then, when I finally got a word in edgeways and I told her how I thought the community centre might well prove to be a bit of a top totty magnet? Well, that really did it! Clare launched straight into the old All Men Are The Same routine and indicated in no uncertain terms that she was never ever going to look at another guy, let alone get involved with one for the rest of her life. But I mean, we all say that, don't we? Yeah, but only for about ten minutes in my case, ha ha ha!!

Steven • JULY 24th

Wow! Just got e-mail from Clare 2 say how not bothered she is by Troy thing. Which is gr8. Really glad 4 her. Really glad 4 me 2 since it was me who told Craig in 1st place! Oh well. No harm done 4tun8ly. Clare v. in2 idea of community centre. Wants 2 meet 2 talk about it! Me meet Clare? Must check calendar. C if Christmas early this year. Can't think what 2 say. Can't think what 2 wear. Can't think full stop. Need 2 talk 2 some1. Need advice what 2 do.

Craig • JULY 24th

You know how they say there's a first time for everything? Well I reckon they're right, whoever <u>they</u> are. Because check this out, as Seb would no doubt say. I've only been asked for some advice about dates and going out with girls and stuff, haven't I? Yeah, I know! The word flippingunbelievable springs to mind! Let's face it, asking me advice about girls is a bit like asking a hedgehog how to cross the road! Of course, I didn't say that to Steven. Oh yeah, it was Steven, by the way. Apparently Clare's asked him out on a hot date! Well, I'm not sure about the hot bit, but frankly any date is hot in my books. Anyway, Clare wants to meet Steven next week at the community centre and now he's worried about what he's going to wear. I don't know if I did the right thing or not, but I suggested he makes a list.

Steven • JULY 25th

1. Woolly hat + anorak.
2. Or not.

Meera • JULY 26th

Dear Leo, hope you're well. I'm obviously not, otherwise I wouldn't be writing to you again. Mandy still thinks it's dead weird that I do this, by the way. That I go on about my various hang-ups and the way I'm feeling and stuff. But it's not like I ever actually send these letters, is it? Doing this acts like a kind of therapy for me and stops too much stuff building up inside which surely has to be a good thing, doesn't it? Besides, it's going to save an absolute fortune in psychiatrists' bills in years to come! 'So why the long face, Meera?' I hear you ask. Well, you know. Stuff. Boyfriend stuff mainly. Or should I say so-called boyfriend stuff? I guess I feel like I'm stuck in a bit of a rut basically. Like my life's on auto-pilot. Like something needs to change? Or some<u>one</u> needs to change, if you get my drift. I think something just needs to happen basically. Maybe the new cybercafé's going to be the answer? Sounds like it might be quite good fun actually. I hear there's even going to be a website. Hey, maybe they'll need someone to help run it? I could do that! Well why not? We've done a bit about web design in computer studies, haven't we? And, let's face it, Leo, I've spent enough time browsing all your sites! Talking of which, gotta go, babe. There's a PC and it's got my name on it!

Seb • JULY 27th

Haven't chilled with Meera for a seriously long time, man. I'm beginning to wonder what the score is between me and her, you know what I'm saying? Right now it seems like she's some kind of virtual girlfriend. Why virtual? Because I virtually never see her, that's why, dude! I've tried calling her loads of times, but I can never get through. Either her line's on the blink or she's been doing some serious surfing lately. I suppose I could always phone Mandy and ask her how Meera's getting on, couldn't I? In a subtle, round about kind of way obviously. Got to maintain my impeccable cool at all times, you know what I'm saying? Can't let on that I'm bothered or anything. Me? The Chickmeister General? Bothered? Yeah right, man. Big up myself basically. Yo! My name is . . . my name is . . . my name is . . . Slim Madely!!

Mandy • JULY 27th

Honestly, what is Seb like? I can read that boy like a book, I really can. Yeah, even if it is a book written in a completely foreign language! He just called. Tried to be dead casual. Like we speak every day or something. He said he just wanted to, you know, chill basically, maaan, and see how it was hanging. I told him not to be so cheeky and that how it was hanging was strictly my business! There was this pause. Like he didn't know what to say next. So I just came straight out with it. I said, look, Seb, if you really want to know how Meera is, why don't you ask her yourself? I told him that she'd probably be at the opening of the cybercafé next week and why didn't he come along too? Which was obviously a mistake on my part because he started ranting on about how community centres were just full of losers playing ping-pong and line dancing. Anyway I happened to mention that the youth worker guy in charge of the community centre was rumoured to be a quality piece of trouser and that I'd be first in the queue for when they opened the doors, or possibly second, depending on whether Meera got there before me or not. That seemed to do the trick. Seb said he'd see me there. I feel a bit rotten about it now, teasing him like that. Let's face it, the probability of this guy really turning out to be a quality piece of trouser is less than zilch. I mean he's bound to be some beardy bloke in sandals and chunky knit sweater on day release from nerd school. Am I right, or am I right?

Steven • JULY 28th

H8 2 admit it, but can't wear woolly hat 2c Clare. Clare much 2 classy. Hat 2 scruffy. Getting old + worn. What 2 do? Don't want 2 blow this. I know. Will get new 1! Steven Stevens UR a genius! Better get looking. Will surf net.

Clare • JULY 28th

OK, so I've had a wee change of mind over this whole community centre cybercafé thing. Well, not so much a wee change of mind as a complete tyre-screeching, rubber-burning, 100% U-turn! So what? This is a democratic society we live in, isn't it? Correct me if I'm wrong, but people are actually allowed to change their minds if they want to, aren't they? And I've changed mine. So sue me! Actually, I still can't pinpoint exactly why I've changed my mind. Oooh, I know, perhaps it's a subconscious decision to attempt to fill the aching void left by Troy's heartless betrayal. Who cares, frankly? What am I, a psychiatrist or something? All that matters is that I think we can make a real go of this cybercafé if we all pull together. It could be extremely rewarding. You know, actually getting off our backsides and doing something instead of sitting back and expecting things to happen. And it could be a good laugh too! Cue fanfare. Time to rally the troops! Now then, who haven't I called yet?

Craig • JULY 29th

I'm not getting too excited about this, I'm really not. Let's face it, I've been here before, haven't I? Several times in fact! Kidded myself that someone's asked me out when they haven't really. Yeah, and I've nearly always ended up looking like a right divvy. But you can hardly blame me for letting my imagination run riot sometimes, can you? You know, given my track record. Or rather lack of it. Until fairly recently even making eye to eye contact with a girl of the opposite, you know, thingy was quite a feat for me. So for Clare to ring me up and for me to actually have a conversation with her for nearly three whole minutes (not that I was counting or anything) and for her to ask to meet me at the community centre is like the next best thing to <u>doing it</u>. Not that I'd know what <u>that</u> was like of course. Hang on. Isn't Clare supposed to be meeting Steven at the community centre as well? See what I mean? See why I'm not getting too excited? Either a) Clare's deliberately trying to stir up tension between me and Steven, or b) there's a perfectly reasonable explanation for all this. Yeah, I know. Tough call, isn't it?

Steven • JULY 30th

Re search 4 new hat. Search now over. Found gr8 website. Called Hat.com. Never knew there were so many different kinds. 'Something 2 suit all tastes' as ad goes. At least £1 cheaper than in shops 2! (Plus post &

packing.) Must decide which sort 2 get. Maybe time 4 change of image? 1der which 1 Clare would like.

Seb • JULY 31st

Look, man, just for the record, I don't feel even remotely threatened by this youth worker dude at the community centre, despite what Mandy says about him being a 'quality piece of trouser'. Yeah, whatever that means! Why chicks can't talk in plain English is like, a total mystery to me basically, man. For real. Mos def. Anyway, I'm presuming that the general gist is that this guy is supposed to be vaguely desirable. Unless, of course, Mandy and Meera are just trying to wind me up and make me jealous. Which would be well ridiculous, obviously. I mean, think about it, man. Me jealous? Listen up, right. Slim Madely does not do jealousy. Look up the word 'jealous' in my dictionary and it says 'see everyone else, dude'. Having said that though, I might just go and check this place out anyway. Strictly out of curiosity, you know what I'm saying? Yeah well, even cutting edge DJs like myself need the occasional break from creating sonic landscapes. And besides, it turns out we're not going away to Devon this summer after all. Seems like money's a bit, you know, tight at the moment what with the lawn being re-turfed and Marjorie wanting a new conservatory. Bummer basically, dude.

August

Mandy • AUGUST 1st

God, I am <u>sooo</u> bored at work. Roll on the end of the holidays, that's all I can say. Yeah, roll on the beginning of next term! <u>That's</u> how bored I am! Mind you, it doesn't exactly help that, whenever I get home and switch the telly on, there's always some programme about a bunch of girls let loose in Ibiza and snogging themselves stupid for a fortnight. Talk about a dream holiday! Talk about <u>any</u> holiday! Anything to get away from flipping Safebury's. It's really beginning to do my head in. Mum said I was sleep-talking the other night. I thought uh-oh, what was I saying? You know, thinking that it was something dead embarrassing? And it was! Yeah, apparently I suddenly sat bolt upright in bed and said 'Price check, kitchen roll, checkout 3 please!' I mean, how sad is that? But that's what the place does for you. That's why I can't wait for Craig to come in and start waffling on about something or other like he did today. Oh god, all that stuff about him and Steven being asked out by Clare! <u>What</u> a scream! Actually, I think there might be a vacancy for a shelf stacker coming up. I should tell Craig about it. I know he was looking for a job. It would be such a laugh. And it could just help keep me sane!

Craig • AUGUST 1st

I really like going into Safebury's and talking to Mandy. Because she's a mate and everything. <u>And</u> she's a girl! But, well, I just wish she didn't laugh at every single thing I said. It's really beginning to get on my nerves, actually. Like today. All I did was tell her about Clare wanting to see me and Steven at the community centre. What's so hysterical about that? I think she thinks I haven't noticed her biting her tongue and trying to stop her shoulders shaking whenever I talk to her. Maybe I should say something next time? But what? Please don't laugh at me because it's making me sad? Yeah right, that'll work, won't it? It's really annoying though. I mean, it's not like I'm trying to be funny. It's not like I'm actually cracking jokes or anything. I'm just talking about, well, stuff basically. Hey, I'd better not tell Mandy that I saw The Girl In The City Shirt go past on a bus on the way back home. She'd probably wet herself.

Meera • AUGUST 2nd

You know I'm beginning to think that Clare's absolutely right. Men <u>are</u> all the same. I mean, how could you, Leo? Just turn up at a premiere with Gwyneth flipping Lopez on your arm like that? And I know you did. I've just seen the pictures in *Hi* magazine! And anyway isn't <u>she</u> supposed to be going out with Brad Pittstop? Well, I hope she dumps you like she dumped him, Leo! Because you're just not worth it. None of you are. Hey, what can I say? It was fun while it lasted. *Ciao*, baby! Talking of fun while it lasted, I wonder if Seb's going to turn up at the opening of the community centre or not? Like I actually care. Mandy seems to think he is though. That was a rotten trick she played on him. But on the other hand, it does kind of suggest that I'm worth being jealous over. He must still like me. Kind of ironic really when you think about it. Because it's way too late for that now. We should be way beyond just liking. We shouldn't still be playing these silly mind games. Not now. We should have moved on. All I ever wanted was a bit of commitment. Not the 'I want to marry you and live happily ever after' kind of commitment. Ohmygod no! Just, you know, normal boyfriend/girlfriend commitment. I mean, surely that's not too much to ask, is it? Well obviously it is. No, you had your chance, Seb. Then another. And another. And you blew the lot, baby!

Clare • AUGUST 2nd

Got my wee cousin Abi coming down from Glasgow to stay with us tomorrow. Well, I say 'wee'. She probably isn't any more. It's ages since we saw each other. In fact, this'll be the first time since we moved here. Boy, is she in for a culture shock or what? If she feels anything like I felt when I arrived she'll think she's just touched down on a completely different planet. Almost like she's taking her first steps in a brand new civilisation. Well, that's if you can actually call Molton Sodbury a civilisation of course! Oh, I know I'm being a bit unfair. But since when did I work for the Molton Tourist Board? Seriously though, it'll be fun having Abi around for a while. It'll be great to have a good blether and catch up on old times and all that. I bet she hasn't changed a bit.

I bet she's still dead shy and quiet. In fact, I bet I won't even know she's around half the time. I still reckon Molton's a weird choice for a summer holiday mind you, but each to their own. I can only think Siberia must be fully booked already!

Steven • AUGUST 3rd

New hat arrived 2day. Just in time 4 seeing Clare 2morrow @ cybercafé. Hat.com defin8ly gr8 idea. £1 cheaper than shops. OK so post + packing cost £1.70 but bus fares would have been 80p. So saved 10p. Result! Saved more wear + tear on boots 2. Double result! Still need new boots though. Maybe search 4 Shoes.com.

Craig • AUGUST 3rd

Well, I take back all that stuff I said about Mandy the other day, because it's thanks to Mandy that I've just got myself a job! OK, so stacking shelves at Safebury's might not be rocket science, but the money's pretty good <u>and</u> it means I get to stay out the house an extra 15 hours a week. Which means 15 fewer hours of being made to feel sick every time I see my parents. I mean, do they really have to keep pawing each other and kissing like that? Isn't that how Mum got to be expecting this flipping baby in the first place? Well, you know, in a roundabout kind of way obviously. I'm not that stupid! I've seen my sister's magazines! Actually, talking about my sister's magazines I was looking at one today and there was this really interesting article in it. Yeah, all about how women find men with a sense of humour dead attractive and all that. Which got me thinking. Maybe it's not such a bad thing that Mandy thinks I'm funny after all. I start at Safebury's on Monday, by the way.

Clare • AUGUST 3rd

Got to keep this short today because Abi's just arrived and we're supposed to be going out. Well, that's if she ever gets out the bathroom. Honestly, as soon as I mentioned we were going into town she was straight in there with her lippy and her mascara! Don't know who she's expecting to meet. Anyway, we're only going for a quick walk. Aye well, Mum said that we're going to be eating an hour from now and why didn't I show my wee cousin Molton's cultural hot spots in the meantime? Which is fine. But I mean, what are we going to do for the other 59 minutes?

Mandy • AUGUST 4th

Well, I can forget spending the rest of my life working at flipping Safebury's! And I can forget the glittering world of showbusiness too! Because I've discovered a hidden talent I never even knew I had! Yeah, starting rumours that turn out to be true! Remember the one I totally made up about the youth worker guy at the community centre being a quality piece of trouser? Oh . . . my . . . god! You should see him! Actually, quality piece of trouser is a gross understatement. You could be done under the Trades Description Act calling him that! No, believe me, this guy is totty of the very highest order. I couldn't tell you anything about the community centre, or the cybercafé, or who was there, or what happened, or any of that stuff. As soon as Jason walked in I was like, woooooooof, steady on, girlfriend!! Think I'll text Meera. See if I missed anything! Yeah, then maybe start a rumour that I've won the Lottery, ha ha!

Meera • AUGUST 4th

Got a text from Mandy a minute ago. JUST :-9 CMNINS which, if I'm not mistaken, is probably meant to translate as Jason Utterly Sex Tastic, I'm licking my lips, Call Me Now If Not Sooner. Of course I know what that'll be about. She'll want to know what she missed at the cybercafé today. You know, what with her eyes being glazed over the whole time and her tongue practically touching the floor. Talk about subtle! Well, I'll call her in a minute because she missed plenty as a matter of fact. Like Seb being there, for a start, trying to act cool but failing miserably. Like Craig cornering me and subjecting me to a load of screamingly unfunny knock knock jokes. Like Clare volunteering to help run the actual café side of things (yeah I know, ohmygod ohmygod, put the hospital on red alert!). Like Clare's cousin Abi seeming really nice. Like some kids from Strange Hill strolling in like they owned the place and sussing us lot out. Like one of them being, well, lush incidentally. Oh, and like Steven's brand new woolly hat being exactly like his old one, just in better nick. Bless!

Seb • AUGUST 4th

Yo! Diary! Check this out, right? Because this community centre might just be cool after all, you know what I'm saying? Actually I'm messing with you, man, because as a matter of fact I think the place is going to be well awesome! Yeah, well I didn't know there was going to be a recording studio and decks and everything, did I? We're talking state of the art gear, dude! I'm going to be able to sample beats and sounds and Steven's going to show me how to download stuff from all these phat music websites he knows about. I tell you, it's going to be wicked, man. Mos def. Big up the community centre basically. Big up the cybercafé too, as a matter of fact, because they do a well hard cappuccino. Still not too sure about the Meera situation though. She was playing it pretty cool today. If I'm being honest there was like, you know, a distinct lack of eye contact going down. As a matter of fact, for some reason Meera seemed to be more interested in the dudes from Strange Hill than she was in The Sebmeister. Yeah, I know. Bizarre but true, man. For real.

Steven • AUGUST 4th

Saw Clare 2day. Went pretty well. Said she liked my hat, anyway. Told her how I got it. Un4tun8 about others being there 2. Oh well. Always next time. Clare's cousin v. nice. Didn't say much. Seemed shy. That's OK though. Can rel8 to that! Since when has shyness been criminal offence? 1ts 2 help Clare run café. 1der if she's veggie 2? Seb v. in2 recording studio etc. Have off4ed 2 help. Detected bit of 10tion when kids from other school turned up. Not sure Y. Seemed OK 2 me.

The community centre really is going to be a great place to hang out this summer. I don't want to sound too much like an advert or anything, but there's so much going on and so much to do. It's brilliant. For a start there's the main hall, with all the lighting and everything. You can do virtually anything with a space like that. I mean apart from the line dancing and table tennis and badminton! We'll be able to put on shows, theatre stuff, discos, you name it really. And, 'of course', it's not just for us lot. There's going to be all kinds of clubs and activities for older folk, as well as crèche facilities for babies and little kids. In other words, there's going to be something for the whole community. Hence the name <u>community</u> centre! Not that it's going to be called that for much longer, hopefully. And I haven't even mentioned the cybercafé yet, have I? Jason, the youth worker guy, was looking for folk to help run the café side of things. And well, I never could resist volunteering for something, could I? Actually, it could be a lot of fun, working out budgets and planning menus and stuff. Maybe do a wee bit of cooking too. Mind you, it's not going to be easy getting that lot to change their eating habits! Oh aye, I forgot to say, didn't I? The café's going to be run on a strictly <u>veggie</u> basis. Naturally.

Craig • AUGUST 4th

Whoa, Clare's cousin is really nice. Such gorgeous eyes and hair and teeth and lips and arms and legs and well, you know, stuff basically. Actually, now I come to mention it, I'm not sure who I like better. Abi, or The Girl In The City Shirt? Who would I choose if they were both up for a bit of a snog, I wonder? If I had the choice, obviously. Yeah right, like <u>that's</u> going to happen! Pity Abi's only going to be here for a few weeks though. But at least I know that I'll be able to find her working at the cybercafé most days. Hey, maybe I should try a few jokes out on her? See if they have any effect. I tried some on Meera today. Purely for research purposes. She obviously thought they were funny. She kept telling me to stop because her sides were splitting. Actually, at this rate I'll soon run out of decent knock knock jokes. I'll just have to start eating more ice lollies, I suppose. You get some absolute crackers on the sticks!

Meera • AUGUST 5th

Wow! Just been talking to Jason about the community centre website and guess what? He's well up for the idea of me helping to run it! Aaaaarrrggghhh!! Me and my big mouth! I just hope I can do it now. Because, I mean, I know a fair bit about the technical side of things from learning about it at school and stuff, but I wouldn't say I'm any kind of expert! Still, Jason seems to know what he's talking about and he says he'll help with the actual setting up side of things. Apparently he's done courses and everything. This is going to be great, I just know it is! I mean, I said I wanted something to happen, didn't I? Well maybe this is it! This is the something! I'm going to get Mandy to help. I mentioned it to Jason. He said yeah, go for it basically and that if we ever got stuck he'd be there for us. Hmm, something tells me that's all the incentive Mandy's going to need!

Mandy • AUGUST 5th

So Captain Testosterone is going to be 'there for us', is he? One word: wooooooooooof!!! OK, so strictly speaking he was just offering to help out with the website-thingy design. But who knows what hidden meaning and cunning subtext there was lurking within that offer? Like anyone up for a bit of tonsil tennis, for instance? Yeah, I know, dream on Mandy! But hey, at least we've got his mobile number now! Actually, I must say that running a website sounds like it might be a bit of a laugh. Not the sort of thing I'd normally get too excited about admittedly. But, well, with Jason being 'there for us', all of a sudden it's a subject I can see myself getting very interested in indeed! And, anyway, anything that can provide a bit of light relief from the sheer drudgery of working at Safebury's has to be a good thing, doesn't it? Talking of which, Craig starts in a couple of days. Hope he's on the same shift as me.

Seb • AUGUST 6th

Listen up, right? Went to the studio at the community centre today. Just to, you know, check the place out basically, you know what I'm saying? Mashed up a few phat sounds. Sussed the gear out some more. I tell you, man, that sampler is well wicked. You can record anything and like, download it on to your PC and play it back and mix it up with your beats or whatever. For real. I can see me giving birth to some truly awesome sonic landscapes, dude. Mos def. There's this one particular tune I'm working on at the moment. It just needs that certain something. Yo, and as soon as I figure out what that certain something is, man, we're in serious business. We're talking the sound of cheque books being waved in my general direction. We're talking record deals, baby. In the meantime, I'm going to suggest we run some kind of regular club night. It'll be well banging. But wait up. Won't we need some totally cutting edge DJ to spin the platters that matter? Hmm, now where can we find one of those round here, dude?

Steven • AUGUST 6th

Had gr8 idea whilst surfing net 2night. How about calling community centre Dot.Com Centre? UC? Com short 4 community! Then we call cybercafé Café Dot.Com! Brilliant. Will suggest it 2 Clare 2morrow if IC her. Or possibly next day. Am xpecting stuff 2 arrive from grimewatch.uk 2morrow. Selection of various cleaning products + free anti-static duster. Couldn't resist. Absolute bargain. Savings of up 2 £1.50 guaranteed. Not including post + packing.

Craig • AUGUST 7th

Well, I was dead right. Stacking shelves at Safebury's is definitely <u>not</u> rocket science. But I'm not going to be doing it forever. Just until I get a bit of money together. And then? Well, actually, I don't know. Doesn't look like we'll be going on holiday this year what with Mum getting so massive and everything. It's probably just as well though. Ugh! Can you imagine her in a swimsuit? She'd look like a flipping beached whale! Some boat would probably come along and tow her back out to sea! And anyway, with any luck, I might have a . . . you know . . . friend of the opposite whatsit before too long. Yeah well, I overheard a couple of girls at work going on about how much they like guys with a sense of humour and all that. So it's obviously true then. Never mind if you're no oil painting, or you're not wearing this week's trainers. Never mind if you prefer Westfield to Coldplace. As long as you're funny you're in with a shout. Which is good news for me, obviously. Actually I'd better go now. Got a lot of jokes to learn from this book I found. And thinking about it, Safebury's sell loads of comedy videos, don't they? Perhaps I should buy one and swot up a bit. Get a few tips from the professionals. After that I just won't be able to fail. God, I should have thought of this years ago!

Clare • AUGUST 7th

Me and Abi went to see Jason today about helping to run the café. Well, I did anyway. Abi just went to flutter her eyelashes, as far as I could tell. Either that or she's got some kind of eye infection. Honestly, the way everybody's going on, you'd think this guy was vaguely attractive or something. Not that I'd know about that, of course, what with me being off men. He thinks that the Dot.Com Centre and Café Dot.Com are great names, by the way. So nice one, Steven! You might be a boy of few words but every one is an absolute gem! Oh, and Jason seems perfectly cool about letting us do pretty much what we want with the place. Within reason, obviously. But, I mean, it's not like we'll be serving five course *cordon bleu* meals or anything. It's only going to be rolls and salads and soup and maybe a hot dish too. I think we'll start off with one of my famous beany stews. Though I say it myself, I do make a mean beany stew!

Seb • AUGUST 8th

Big shout goes out to Jason the community centre guy, dude. Because he's like, given the green light to my idea of a regular club night. Yo! Respect! Big up Jason basically. Not only that, but he went and offered me the gig there and then, man! Before I could even say anything about wanting to do it myself! Seems he was checking out my turntable skills the other day and liked what he heard. Yeah, I know, *quelle surprise*, dude. I mean, who wouldn't basically? Still, it's nice to know the cat's got taste after all, because you know, I was beginning to wonder. I mean calling the place the Dot.Com Centre? I still say my suggestion of the Dead Centre was much better and much more relevant too, what with it being an old converted church <u>and</u> being in the dead centre of town. Oh well, getting the club night is a real result! We start mashing it up this weekend. Just need a name for that sucker now. Something suitably kicking and banging. Mos def.

Meera • AUGUST 9th

Was talking websites with Mand in Café.Com today and who do you suppose was there too? The guy from Strange Hill. The well lush one! Sat there with a couple of mates he was. You know, having a coffee, chatting on his mobile, having a bit of a laugh. Now, I don't know if I'm maybe reading too much into this or not, but at one point he definitely looked in my direction. For a good few seconds. He even took his shades off. Actually he's got really nice eyes. Not that I could see what colour they were or anything. But there were two of them, which is always a plus in my book. And yeah, OK, he could have just been looking over my shoulder at the menu on the wall, but I like to think there was a bit of contact going on as well. Which is more than can be said for when Seb walked in, by the way. I don't think he even knew I was there. He was too busy sticking posters up on every available bit of wall space. Oh, and if anyone can tell me what exactly 'Mashin' Impossible' is, and who exactly 'Special guest DJ Esinem' is, I'd be most grateful. Answers on a postcard to the usual address please.

Mandy • AUGUST 9th

Doing this website definitely sounds like it could be fun. Me and Meera had a meeting about it today and, as an added bonus, the lovely Jason came and sat with us too! Which, on the one hand, meant that it was a bit difficult for me to concentrate without drooling all over the table like a complete divvy but, on the other, meant that we were actually able to discuss what exactly we want to do and how exactly we want to do it. So anyway, there's going to be like a general home page kind of thing with loads of information about the Dot.Com Centre and what we're up to and stuff. Then there'll be a message board and a forum-type-thingy, and links for all the community centre activities. And those of us that want to can have our own pages. So I'm going to write a sort of opinion piece about anything I want to really. Might be something quite heavy. Or it might just be a bit of goss. Who knows? I think Meera's going to do some kind of astrology/ agony aunt thing. Not sure about the others. Jason was saying that Seb might want to download some of his 'kicking beats' and 'phat sounds' so that anyone out there can hear them too, though quite why they'd want to do that is beyond me frankly! Unless, of course, they wanted to use them as a form of torture. Oh, and there's going to be a web cam too. Better make sure there's always a bit of mascara and some lippy next to it. Well, a girl's got to look her best, hasn't she? Ha ha!!

Steven • AUGUST 9th

In Safebury's 2day. Checking out prices of yoghurt. Can get it 2p cheaper (+ post + packing) @ Yog.com. Defin8ly worth it if U get 12 boxes or more. Saw Craig there. Cool uni4m. Talked about this + that. Mainly that. Think Craig is down in dumps. Kept 1ting 2 no if I knew NE good jokes. Didn't. Will think of sum.

Craig • AUGUST 10th

Was talking to Mandy at work today about the Dot.Com Centre and stuff. Her and Meera are busy setting up the website at the moment. Mandy seems to think it's going to be really brilliant and was generally giving it the big sell. Or 'big upping' it, as I believe Seb would say. Personally I'm not so sure though. I happen to think that people who spend their whole lives on the net are like the trainspotters for the new millennium. Just a theory of course. Perhaps I should have kept it to myself, I don't know. Mandy obviously thought it was the funniest thing she'd ever heard though. So I tried out a joke on her. You know, seeing as I was on a bit of a roll. Told her about this bloke who walks into a cybercafé and asks for a pint of cyber. Nothing. Completely stony faced. That's the last time I ask Steven if he knows any jokes!

Steven • AUGUST 10th

Oops. 4got I don't like yoghurt. 1der if it's 2 l8 to cancel? No, will leave it 4 now. It's a bargain. So much cheaper online. 1der how long yoghurt keeps? Can mayb u's 4 Christmas presents.

Clare • AUGUST 10th

I'm glad to say the old beany stew seems to be going down a treat so far. Well, with Steven it is anyway! Honestly, he must have had at least four portions today! Can that boy eat or what? I wouldn't be surprised if he was just being polite though. He's very sweet, Steven. Actually I think Abi's taken a bit of a shine to him. Mind you, I suppose it was only a matter of time. She seems to have taken a bit of a shine to every other guy round here already! Aye, especially Seb! I mean each to their own and all that. And as far as I know Seb and Meera aren't strictly speaking 'an item' any more so theoretically at least he's up for grabs. But even so, I really feel I ought to warn her. After all, she's my wee cousin. It's my duty to protect her from the big bad world and all that. I mean, she's just so young and sweet and innocent. And he's just . . . just . . . well, let's face it, he's just Seb, isn't he? Enough said really!

Seb • AUGUST 11th

Yo! Check this out, right, because there have been more sightings of the Strange Hill Massive down at the Dot.Com Centre lately. Which, by the way, is totally cool with me. Mos def. Because it's a free world, man. Dudes can chill where they want to, you know what I'm saying? And that's all they are doing, by the way. Chilling. Some people might interpret what they're doing as being a bit, you know, provocative. Like they're trying to muscle in on our territory or something. Not me though, man. And besides, it's not our 'territory' in the first place. Just because they come from the other side of town doesn't mean to say they can't hang round here if they want to. Yo! That was a <u>partly</u> political broadcast on behalf of the Seb Party. And talking of party, dude, the posters for Mashin' Impossible seem to be creating the desired buzz. I saw quite literally several people stop and look at them today, you know what I'm saying? Yo! And the word on the street currently is, who is this mysterious guest DJ, Esinem?

Meera • AUGUST 11th

So, www.dotcomcentre.com it is then! Cor, our very own website! How fab is that? Of course, it's early days yet but it's starting to look really good. Dead groovy and colourful. It might even look a bit too colourful! We're talking fluorescent oranges and greens here! Definitely not to be viewed first thing in the morning on an iffy stomach. Not without shades anyway! And bizarrely, although it's only just up and running, we've had a few hits already! Goodness knows how or why though. I mean we haven't advertised at all. What must people have been searching for to come up with us? Unless there's a place in Thailand or somewhere called Dot Khom?! Anyway I've posted my first 'Ask Meera' page. We'll see what happens. See if I get any questions. See if anyone leaves a message on the message board too. Oh, and Mandy's done her first piece. All about this theory she's got how people who spend their whole lives on the net are like the trainspotters for the new millennium. Dead funny it is. Honestly, I don't know how she comes up with this stuff!

Craig • AUGUST 12th

I really don't know whether to be miffed or flattered. I think I might be a bit of both actually. Miffed that Mandy's ripped me off word for word and not even credited me. But at the same time flattered that she thinks I was worth ripping off in the first place. I never knew I could be that profound! I feel like Oscar flipping Wilde or somebody! Maybe I'll leave a message for her on the message board. Give her a hard time about it. Then it's back to the comedy videos I guess. I'm steadily working my way through them, but there's still plenty to go. It's all in a good cause though, isn't it? Well, hopefully it is anyway. Clare and Abi came into

Safebury's today, by the way. Abi looked really nice as usual. I wish I had the bottle to try out some jokes on her. But it wasn't the right time. Judging by the amount of red kidney beans they bought I'd say they were stocking up for Café Dot.Com. I'm sure it's very nice, Clare's beany stew. Steven certainly seems to like it. It's just that, well, I wonder if she knows any other recipes besides that one.

Mandy • AUGUST 12th

Ooh, watch out World because Craig's hopping mad! Honestly what is that boy like? He can't even act cross without coming over as being essentially sweet and funny. At least, I'm pretty sure he was trying to be cross, leaving that message. What was it again? Oh yeah, 'There's only one thing worse than credit not being given where credit's due – and that's being run over by a bus'. Yeah, I know, pretty scary, eh? Point taken though. It won't happen again. Well, not unless I get really stuck for something to write, of course, ha ha!! Not that there's too much danger of that happening, mind you. I've got the title of my next piece sorted already as a matter of fact. 'To Bean Or Not To Bean?' It's all about certain individuals' obsession with inflicting their freaky crank ways on others. Mentioning no names of course! But I mean, my god, if Steven eats any more of that stuff he's surely going to explode! It's like, every time the guy walks in a room the levels of greenhouse emissions and global warming go completely haywire! In fact, we really ought to put a sign round his neck. 'No naked flames!' I mean, think about it. The consequences could be catastrophic!

Steven • AUGUST 13th

Café Dot.Com 4 lunch. Again. Clare's beany s2 gr8 as usual. Clare seemed 2 appreci8 gift as well. Glad 2B of service. Looking 4ward 2 Mashin' Impossible 2morrow. No1 seems 2 no who Esinem is. No1 but me! Esinem = Es + em = S + M = Seb Madely = Seb! It's bl8antly obvious. 2 me anyway.

Clare • AUGUST 13th

Look, I don't want to sound ungrateful or anything, but what exactly is the cybercafé supposed to do with twelve whacking great boxes of yoghurt anyway? I mean, it was very thoughtful of Steven but, let's face it, there's a limit to what anyone can do with the stuff. Mind you, apparently it was an absolute bargain. Steven reckons it's amazing what you can save shopping online. Which is fine if you've got the time <u>and</u> the patience.

Personally I've got neither. I usually get bored out of my mind long before I get anywhere near where I want to get on the net. Or distracted more like. I was browsing and searching for 'driving tips' the other day – I've just got a date for my test by the way – and, well, it was obviously just a slip of the fingers, but I ended up on this site all about 'diving trips'! And from there, there were all these links to holiday destinations and all that. And it got me thinking how great it would be to get away for a wee while. See what I mean? One minute I'm looking to brush up my driving technique and the next I'm mentally packing bags and halfway to the airport!

Seb • AUGUST 13th

Cracked it, dude. That certain something I was searching for for that particular tune of the banging and kicking variety? Turns out it was right under my nose at the Dot.Com Centre the whole time, man! Who would've thought that a ping-pong ball being hit backwards and forwards across a table tennis table could sound so phat and phunky? Well, after it's been sampled and tweaked and distorted a bit. But I want to give my man, Steven, a big shout for suggesting it. It's made all the difference, dude. We're talking sonic landscapes of truly epic proportions here. This tune really is a guaranteed floor filler. Put it this way. If this baby doesn't have the crowd dancing themselves into a heaving frenzy and crying out for mercy tomorrow night then I'm going to be an accountant. Not that I'm dissing accountants or anything. Yo! Big up the Accountancy Massive, you know what I'm saying? For real. Just one more thing to do now then. Just one more thing before Slim Madely well and truly ROCKS the joint! Mos def!

Meera • AUGUST 14th

I wonder if it would be a bit sad to ask myself a question on my web page? Dear Me, what exactly did I ever see in Seb in the first place? How did we actually manage to go out with each other for as long as we did? And what on earth does he think he looks like with that shaved peroxide head of his? OK, so strictly speaking that's three questions. But, I mean, ohmygod ohmygodohmygod!! It was embarrassing enough him and my dad 'DJ-ing' together that time, but tonight I thought he took embarrassment to a whole different level. Of course, that's just my opinion. Other people might have a different opinion. Yeah, but I'd still be right! I mean, come on, Seb, face the facts. You live in a nice house in a totally unremarkable little town. Your dad's a teacher and your mum's a doctor. The furthest west you've ever been was that camping holiday in Cornwall for goodness sake! So tell me something. What's with all the hand gestures and the fake, whiny American accent and all that Slim Madely stuff? Because you're in severe danger of making a complete laughing stock of yourself, Seb. Oops. Some news just in. You just did!

Craig • AUGUST 14th

First night of Mashin' Impossible tonight and already I can't wait till the next one! Why? Well it's not because of the music for a start! Honestly, I don't know what planet Seb's on but it's certainly not this one. I mean, what's with all this Esinem thing? Who's he trying to kid? Sorry, what was I saying? Oh yeah. Can't wait till next Saturday. Well, with any luck she might be there again. Who? The Girl In The City Shirt, that's who! She was there tonight, looking as lovely and as fragrant as ever. Well, actually, I'm not sure about the fragrant bit. I didn't get that close. But she was definitely looking lovely. The only trouble was she was hanging around with a bunch of kids from Strange Hill for some reason. Unless, of course, she actually goes to Strange Hill. Surely not. She seems so nice! I wonder what her name is anyway. And where she lives. Yeah, and whether she's got a, you know, friend of the opposite thingy or not. Because if she hasn't . . . well, put it this way, I'm going to be up all hours, between now and next weekend, studying all my comedy videos and brushing up on my jokes! I'll have her in absolute hysterics! She won't be able to resist! Well, at least that's the theory anyway. Better get cracking I suppose. No time to lose.

Mandy • AUGUST 14th

Phwoar!! Not only is Jason 100% SOAS (that's Sex On A Stick for the terminally unhip), but he can <u>really</u> dance too! I don't know why, but I'd automatically assumed that a youth worker would dance like the proverbial geography teacher at a PTA disco. But no. This boy definitely knows how to shake his booty!! And, boy, was he shaking it tonight or what? Yeah, the only trouble was, he was too busy shaking it in the direction of some over-made-up floozy to notice me. Oh well. I was quite happy just browsing! I mean, wooooof! Ooh, I can feel a text coming on. I wonder if Meera's still up. She's bound to be. She recorded 'Celebrity Chef Castaways From Hell' like I did. Which reminds me, I still haven't watched that new programme where ordinary members of the public get to do nothing of interest whatsoever. God, I'm never going to get to bed at this rate and I've got work in the morning. And, I mean, I've really got to be alert and on the ball for that, haven't I? If I wasn't, who knows what chaos might ensue? I could be on the 9 Items Or Less checkout and accidentally let someone with 10 items through! Yeah, I know, hold the front page, ha ha!!

Clare • AUGUST 14th

Honestly, I wish I'd known tonight was supposed to be fancy dress. It was really embarrassing, turning up in my ordinary clothes like that. Mind you, everybody else obviously forgot as well. Aye, everybody except Seb that is. He really made an effort too, bless him, what with the blond hair, the dungarees, the ice hockey mask and the temporary tattoo. I'm not exactly sure but I think he might have been trying to look like someone vaguely hip and trendy and streetwise. Someone 'down with the kids', as I believe the saying goes. On the other hand, he might just have been trying to look like a complete divvy. In which case, well, result basically, Seb! Honestly, to think that once upon a time he and I might have . . . well, let's leave it at that, shall we? We might have. But I was so much younger then. Well OK, only 18 months younger. But I was an innocent wee lassie then. Just arrived frae bonny Scotland and all that. Just like my wee cousin Abi really. It was quite sweet to see her tonight actually. Just watching. Taking it all in. And she was obviously fooled by Seb's disguise! I mean how naive is that? Esinem my arm!

Seb • AUGUST 14th

Stormed it, man. Totally blew the place away basically. Like putty in my hands they were. I tell you, it was like the Valentine's Disco all over again. Yeah, only this time it was even more awesome, dude! And yeah, sure I played all the poppy charty stuff to begin with. Just to, you know, get everyone on their feet. But then I hit them with a specially extended mix of my latest grooves and tunes, <u>including</u> the one with the ping-pong beats and well, what can I say? The whole crowd were just, like totally gobsmacked and awe-struck. So much so that they all just sat down as one and listened. Just like that, man. It was incredible! And then? Well, as soon as I finished everyone clapped and cheered and basically big upped me. Then as soon as I started playing all the poppy charty stuff again everyone got back up and started dancing! I tell you, man, it's amazing to have so much power at your fingertips. Quite a buzz. I mean, I knew I was good, but I didn't know I was <u>that</u> good! Yo! Mashin' Impossible? Mission accomplished, dude! Mos def.

Steven • AUGUST 15th

Club last night defin8ly gr8 success. At least according 2 Seb, aka Esinem, aka Slim Madely. Will have 2 take his word 4 it. Personally only got as far as Café Dot.Com. Only 1 other person there. Guy from Strange Hill. Sat next 2 me. We chatted 4 while. Not face 2 face but in chatroom. Discovered his name is David Davids. Suspect we might have a lot in common. Will perhaps make list. Have arranged to chat again. PS, Cold beany s2 surprisingly nice.

Craig • AUGUST 15th

Girl In The City Shirt
you make my brain hurt
you make my heart pound
you make my blood go round
ensuring a good supply
of oxygen to my vital organs and that's why
I don't die
and it's all thanks to you
my love in shirt
of white and blue.

Meera • AUGUST 15th

Met Mandy in Café Dot.Com for lunch today. I use the term 'lunch' loosely by the way. The only thing on the menu (apart from flipping beany stew, of course) was 'home-made flapjack'. Little did I know that what this actually meant was flapjack quite literally made out of bits of Clare's home . . . hoover fluff, stuff from down the back of the sofa, toenail clippings, that kind of thing. Yum! And talk about chewy! All washed down with a nice cup of herbal tea. Camomile and privet hedge I think it was called. I must say I'm not normally a big fan of herbal tea. Yeah, and now I know why. It was absolutely disgusting! Mind you, the alternative was organic prune juice! I wonder if the Health Police would notice if I sneaked a can of Coke in. Abi certainly noticed Seb when he came in. You should've seen those eyelashes flutter! Which just goes to show there really is no accounting for taste. Anyway, it was good to see Mand and have a bit of a goss. Actually, she seemed a bit miffed that I hadn't replied to a message she'd sent me. The funny thing is though, I haven't received any messages lately.

Mandy • AUGUST 15th

That's it! The next time I have lunch at Café Dot.Com I'm going for a burger first! Get some proper food down me. I mean, how much longer have we got to put up with this? Why should Clare be allowed to inflict her frankly weird ways on us? If it was the other way round she'd soon have something to say about it. It's not just me that feels like this either. Meera's exactly the same. By the way, am I imagining things or was Meera just a teensy bit jealous today? When Abi was blatantly flirting with Seb. I wouldn't blame her if she was, mind you. I'd probably be a bit jealous myself. I mean, those two were an item, on and off, until . . . well, until it just kind of fizzled out basically. Hard to put a date to it. They didn't officially ever break up. So I don't suppose it's that surprising if Meera bristled a bit when she clocked what was happening. Of course, Seb didn't have a clue what was going on. Let's face it, he very rarely does! Honestly, you could gyrate in front of that boy licking your eyebrows and he still wouldn't get the message! And talking of messages, how come Meera never got my text? I'm sure I sent it.

Clare • AUGUST 16th

Blimey O'Reilly, if I'd known it was going to be that easy I would've brought the subject up a long time ago. I only got as far as 'Dad, you know how they say that travel broadens the mind?' and he basically said no problem, where do you fancy going? Aye, just like that! I think he really wants to go away himself. And now Mum's packed in her summer school there's nothing to stop us! Anyway, I mumbled something or other about looking into it. Actually, I think I might ask Steven to give me a hand, browsing the net and all that. Let's face it, if anyone knows where to find a last minute bargain it'll be Steven! Aw, this is going to be great! I wonder where we can go. I say 'we'. That's me, my folks <u>and</u> Abi of course. I've always fancied Barcelona myself. Or maybe Florence. Somewhere dead cultural and that. The museums, the galleries, the architecture. Sipping cappuccinos in some little café, reading my book and watching the world go by. Which reminds me. I suppose I'll have to get someone else to help out at Café Dot.Com while I'm away. Shouldn't be a problem. I still can't quite believe it. Actually I'm beginning to feel a wee bit guilty now. I mean, it's not that long since my folks bought me the car, is it? Perhaps I should tell them I've changed my mind and that I think I should stay at home instead. Yeah right!

Craig • AUGUST 16th

Any minute now I'm expecting to wake up and have one of those 'phew to think it was all a dream' moments they have on the telly or in kids' books. Why? I only talked to The Girl In The City Shirt today, didn't I? That's right. Actually talked to her! In Safebury's. I'll never forget. Aisle number 5 it was. I was stacking tinned fruit, I turned round and there she was! She said, 'Do you have lychees?' Of course, I now realise that what I should have said was, 'No, I always walk like this.' I didn't though. I just said, 'Yeah' and pointed them out to her. OK, so it wasn't brilliant, but I mean it's a start, isn't it? Maybe next time I'll try a joke out on her. And I'm pretty sure there will be a next time. Because she definitely said, 'Thanks. See you.' Unless, of course, it was more of a general 'see you'. I don't think so though. It was almost like there was a question mark at the end. You know like, 'See you?' In other words, 'Can I see you?' Or in other other words, 'Let's you and me get horizontal sometime, baby.' Hmm, maybe not. But she did definitely say, 'See you.' I think I'm going to have to have a lie down.

Mandy • AUGUST 16th

Aaaaaaarrghh!! So that's why Meera never got my text! I accidentally sent it to Jason instead!! Yeah well, his number's in my directory, isn't it? And I guess I must have forgotten to lock the keypad and the phone must have been rattling around in my bag and the send button got pressed or something. Oh, anyway, it happened! And considering that the subject of the text was none other than Mr Lovepants himself, the consequences could have been pretty flipping horrendous, not to mention horrifically embarrassing. But, thanks to a bit of quick thinking from yours truly, I got away with it. Or at least I think I did, anyway! Yeah well, Jason called me into his office today to ask what SOAS meant!! Straight off the top of my head and quick as a flash I told him it stood for Showcase On After Summer! Yeah I know, pretty implausible but it was all I could think of at the time! The next thing Jason's going, 'Hmm, interesting, Mandy. Go on,' and before I knew it I was rambling on about how we could hold this sort of Big-Bash-Talent-Night-Concert-Type-Thing before the end of the holidays! The funny thing was though, once I'd said it, it actually sounded like a pretty good idea! So we're going to do it! I know. Weird or what?

Seb • AUGUST 17th

That was most uncool of Clare today in the café, man. And totally unnecessary too, you know what I'm saying? All Abi did was like, ask if she could look at my decks sometime. Perfectly understandable, dude. I mean, she's just a young chick basically. Fresh down from Scotland. Probably lives on some remote heather-covered mountainside, overlooking a loch. Probably spends most of her life listening to bagpipes and watching her dad toss cabers. Almost definitely never heard kicking tunes and phat beats like mine before. Who can blame her if she's curious? I'd be curious too if I was her. So, I really don't know what Clare was doing, steaming in like that, trying to change the subject and talking about holidays and that. Almost like I was trying to corrupt her little cousin or something. The kid obviously just wanted to chill with someone a bit more street, that's all. Just wanted to taste inner city life for herself instead of reading about it in some magazine, you know what I'm saying? Which reminds me. Dad – sorry, Dennis – has promised that if I weed the rockery once a week he'll pay for a subscription to *Phunk Phortnightly*. Big up Dennis basically. Respect due.

Steven • AUGUST 17th

In Café Dot.Com all day 2day looking 4 holidays on net. Not 4 me. 4 Clare + Abi. Couple of possibilities so far:

1. Canals + Rivers Of The Midlands and North West England. A 4tnight of meandering round some of

Britain's most fascin8ing navigable waterways with a wide choice of fully equipped longboats + luxury cabin cruisers. A must 4 lovers of nice scenery, industrial heritage + not going very fast. Or . . .

2. 7 nights in Ibiza.
Clare v. gr8ful. Let me eat as much beany s2 as I 1ted! 1der which they'll go 4? Know which I'd prefer. But then I've always had a thing 4 boats.

Meera • AUGUST 17th

Ohmygodohmygod! How embarrassing must that have been for Mandy?! Talk about quick thinking though! Must have been the actress in her, I suppose. Honestly, what is she like? Showcase On After Summer indeed! But she's right. It is a pretty damn good idea! It'll be something for everybody to get involved in. Something to focus on. Something to look forward to. And the more stuff I've got to look forward to the better, as far as I'm concerned, what with there currently being a vacancy in the boyfriend department. Not that I'm bothered or anything. Because I'm not. Abi can pout at Seb all she wants. I couldn't care less. Personally I can't be doing with all that relationship stuff at the moment. I'm perfectly happy to dish advice out though! Actually

I got this really sweet e-mail today on my Ask Meera page from some guy just calling himself Confused Of Molton. Apparently this girl he fancies said 'see you' to him. So far he's interpreted this in about seventeen different ways but still doesn't know what to do. Maybe I should write back and tell him that what he really needs to do is get out more. There you go. Sorted! Piece of cake this!

Clare • AUGUST 18th

Well, predictably there's been a wee difference of opinion re the ongoing choice of holiday situation. Basically my folks don't want to do what I want to do and vice versa. But, at the end of the day, we had to make a decision. It wasn't exactly something we could compromise on. It was either canals or Ibiza. So, we flipped a coin. And my parents won. So, Ibiza it is then. God, anyone would think holidays were for enjoying yourself or something! Oh well, as long as I get to choose next time. Mind you, Abi's dead excited. But then she's that much younger than me. As far as she's concerned it's going to be two solid weeks of sun, sand, sea, clubbing and snogging, which frankly sounds like hell if you ask me. Especially the snogging part, since I'm still off men. Actually I'm beginning to think that maybe Abi isn't quite so sweet and innocent as I'd thought. I'll have to watch her. And if that means me having to go clubbing too, well then, that's the price I'll have to pay. As long as she doesn't mind coming along to museums and galleries in the daytime with me. That's fair enough, isn't it?

Mandy • AUGUST 18th

Café Dot.Com seems to be going really brilliantly at the moment. Well, at least the Dot.Com bit is. Loads of people browsing the net, hitting the website and leaving messages and stuff. Not sure the café bit's going quite so well, mind you. In fact, if it wasn't for Steven Stevens I don't think the café bit would be going at all! I wonder if Steven's twigged why he always seems to be able to get a table to himself these days. It's because of all the flipping beany stew he's been consuming, that's why! I tell you, that boy's a one man walking ridge of high pressure. Approach at your peril, if you get my drift. Someone should tell him. Well, that's if they dare get close enough, of course. It's either that or we think of some way to halt production of the dreaded concoction in the first place. But how could we do that? Hmm, time to set the rumour mill in motion again, I think.

Craig • AUGUST 18th

Got a reply from Meera on the website. She said that what I really need to do is forget about ever getting a girlfriend once and for all and to go round wearing a T-shirt with 'Big Girlie Virgin' printed on it for the rest of my life. Nah, she didn't really. But I bet that's what she thinks every time she sees me. Except, of course, that she doesn't actually know that I'm Confused Of Molton. I'd die of embarrassment if she did. She did reply though. Well, kind of. She asked me what star sign I was and recommended that I try putting a few drops of lavender oil in my bath last thing at night. Yeah, she said it had nothing whatsoever to do with my question, but that it might help me relax more. Relax? Me? Three days away from (hopefully) seeing The Girl In The City Shirt again and with a whole stack of comedy videos and joke books still to get through! And she's talking about relaxing? Oh, what the heck. I'll give anything a go once.

Steven • AUGUST 19th

David Davids at Café Dot.Com 2day. We chatted online again 4 a while. Seems like nice bloke. V. in2 thrash & metal. Got guitar but only plays in room. Told me about gr8 site to download music from. Stuff like Slipsnot +

Mama Roach. I told him about site where U can buy really cheap stationery. Up 2 50% off pencils 4 limited period only (plus post + packing). Decided not 2 eat 2day. Not after seeing message on message board.

Clare • AUGUST 19th

Eh? This has got to be a wind-up, hasn't it? I mean, come on. Mad Courgette Disease?! First I've heard about it. Well, I don't know. Just because some rumour appeared on the website doesn't mean it's true, does it? Or does it? Perhaps I ought to stop putting them in the stew anyway. You know, just in case. Just to be on the safe side. I mean, I'm sure there's nothing in it, but then I'd never forgive myself if something happened, would I? And I have to say, the side effects do sound pretty awful. Increased introversion, lack of communicative skills, severe build-up of bodily gases. Oh my god, I've just described Steven Stevens! Perhaps there really is something to this after all! Thinking about it, Steven was sat at that PC virtually all day today and never said a word. No change there then. But the only person who came anywhere near him was that guy from Strange Hill. (Honestly, they could pass for twins those two, in their combat jackets and matching woolly hats.) Hmm, well that's that then. From now on it's Beany Stew À *La*

Clare *Sans* Courgettes. But the stew <u>will</u> go on! Oh yes. It will go on!

Seb • AUGUST 19th

All systems go for this week's Mashin' Impossible, man. Just been putting the finishing touches to another totally massive tune. With a little bit of help from my main man Steven, as a matter of fact. Yo, check this out right, because Steven came up with this well wicked idea of sampling the sound of all these dudes line dancing in the Dot.Com Centre. You know, the bit where they all touch their ankles, spin round and then clap their hands? Now, in the hands of a mere mortal, that could end up sounding seriously naff basically. But, in the capable hands of yours truly, DJ Sebsonic, aka The Groovemaster General, aka The Real Slim Madely, there's precisely no chance of that happening, you know what I'm saying? For real. Yo, remember where you heard it first, man. Line dancing rocks! Which is more than can be said for online chatrooms, by the way. Steven keeps telling me I should give it a go. Now if it was anyone else I'd tell them thanks very much but that I already have a life. But, like I say, Steven's my man. I don't want to hurt his feelings. Wouldn't hurt to do it once, would it?

Meera • AUGUST 20th

Was that really Seb I saw, glued to a PC in Café Dot.Com today? It was a bit hard to tell, what with the hood and the shades, but I'm pretty sure it was. Will wonders never cease? Because, I mean, I thought that kind of thing was way too nerdy and uncool for Seb. The internet? Isn't that something that like, you know, ordinary people do? Maaaaaaan. Just got another question on my web page from Confused Of Molton, by the way. Who I now know is Capricorn. So no wonder he's confused, what with the sun being in Taurus at the moment. Anyway he wants to know where he can buy some lavender oil to put in his bath. Nice to know my advice is being taken seriously. Mind you, I think he might be a bit of a joker on the side, old Confused, because he also wants to know if I can recommend anything for nausea? Yeah, apparently every time he sees his parents he feels sick!

Craig • AUGUST 20th

Good grief, just how much bigger is my mum going to get before she has this flipping baby? Honestly, she's the size of a bus already! I tell you, she'd better not stand too close to a double yellow line because sooner or later some warden's going to slap a ticket on her. I'm not

73

kidding, she came into Safebury's today and people were having to turn sideways to get past her in the aisles. Cheers for that, by the way, Mum. You obviously don't think I've suffered quite enough public humiliation recently. Not that we were actually seen together at any time. What am I, crazy or something? I was hiding in the back of the store, watching the whole thing on CCTV! I don't know what she said to Mandy at the checkout, by the way, but it was obviously highly amusing. Mandy could hardly keep a straight face the next time she saw me. What next? Mum to come and pick me up from Mashin' Impossible tomorrow night? I wouldn't put it past her!

Mandy • AUGUST 20th

Poor old Craig. He was in absolute bits today, his mum coming into the store like that. Honestly I've never seen him move so fast. But, boy, was it funny or what? Actually, it's a good job he was hiding in the back. I'm not sure what he would have done if he'd heard me on the tannoy going 'Maternity pants, price check – checkout 5 please!' Don't get me wrong, working in Safebury's still sucks big-time, but it's been a lot less boring since Craig's been around! His mum's really nice too. Always asks me how I am and stuff. Always tells me how she keeps expecting to see me on the telly. Yeah, I know, must be her hormones raging out of control or something, because there's not much chance of <u>that</u> happening at the moment! Actually she seemed quite concerned about Craig. Says he's been up really late at night, pacing around his bedroom and talking to himself. She asked me if I'd noticed him behaving oddly recently. I'm still not sure if, 'How long have you got?' was the most diplomatic of answers!

Meera • AUGUST 21st

Ohmygodohmygodohmygod, I have <u>so</u> got to text Mandy!! The problem is though, how exactly do I manage to say that the moment I clapped eyes on the lush guy from Strange Hill at Mashin' Impossible tonight, looking unbelievably fit and generally drop-dead gorgeous, like a cross between Ronnie Williams and What's-his-face from FClub Heaven, I had this overwhelming urge to leap on top of him and forcibly try to remove his tonsils using only my tongue . . . in 40 characters or less? I don't think I can, basically. Maybe I'll phone instead. Once I've calmed down a bit and can actually string a couple of words together, obviously. Honestly, though, I'm not going to get too carried away. Just because he absolutely definitely, very nearly, almost smiled at me at one point doesn't mean he fancies me or anything. Does it? No, course it doesn't. So I'm playing this one cool. Ohmygodohmy godohmygod! Well, cool<u>ish</u>!

Clare • AUGUST 21st

Sweet and innocent?! My wee cousin?! Abi?! Hell-oo!! Earth to Clare! Come in please, Clare! I tell you, what I witnessed tonight in the studio was most definitely <u>not</u> sweet and innocent! In fact, what I witnessed tonight in the studio was bordering on the downright disgusting, if you ask me! I'm not kidding, it was like something you see on the Discovery Channel in there! OK, so maybe I am exaggerating just a wee bit. They were only snogging. But, the point is, another couple of seconds and who knows what they might have got up to? No, if you ask me I reckon it was a good job I walked in when I did. Think of it as my good deed for the day. My bit of community service. Preventing something they would have both ended up regretting. Well, she would anyway! In fact, thinking about it he probably led her on in the first place. Despite the fact that she seemed to have him pinned up against the wall. I mean, looks can be deceptive and all that. Aye, that's it. He was the instigator all along! It's obvious now when I think about it. I feel terrible. How could I ever have doubted her? My own wee cousin. Wee Abi.

Seb • AUGUST 21st

What can I say, man? She virtually threw herself at me! Took me completely by surprise. For real! One minute I'm showing her the sampler and the next she's saying 'sample <u>this</u>, baby' and you know, giving it some serious face to face resuscitation! I was powerless to resist. Literally, man. Yo, listen up, right, because for a small chick, Abi's a lot stronger than she looks. Must be all that porridge they eat up in Scotland or something. Whatever. I tell you what though, man, not only was the whole experience a bit of a throat opener, it was a bit of an eye opener as well, you know what I'm saying? Well, let's face it, it's been a while, dude. You know, since me and Meera . . . well, like I say, it's been a while, dude. And once the initial surprise had worn off, I really started to get into it. It was well pleasant basically. Just a pity Clare walked in when she did. But it's made me think, man. Maybe I've been a bit too focused on banging beats and sonic cathedrals lately. I mean, I can still do all that. But why ignore the obvious, man? Once a chick magnet, <u>always</u> a chick magnet! Nuff said. Seb out.

Steven • AUGUST 21st

Mashin' Impossible really gr8. Seb's essential mix of drum 'n' house 'n' line dance especially good. V. long 2. Seb disappeared 4 20 minutes. Still going on when he got back! Strange Hill mob there in 4ce. Including David Davids. Both head banging 2 Damp Bizkit! Didn't chat 2nite though. Will do that in Café Dot.Com next time.

Craig • AUGUST 21st

Yes! You beauty! My mum never turned up at the club tonight, thank god! But The Girl In The City Shirt did! Yes! And we spoke! Yes! Yes!! And I tried a couple of jokes out on her. And, well, she didn't exactly throw herself at me and stick her tongue down the back of my throat. But she smiled. She definitely smiled! Yes! Yes!! Yes!!! Baby, baby, baby, come to Craigy!! She did laugh out loud at one point, but I think she must have misheard me, what with the volume of the music and everything. Because, I mean, all I said was, 'Fancy a dance?' But I definitely feel like it's all starting to pay off. This sense of humour thing. It really does seem to work! All I've got to do now is find out her name and then? Well, who knows what might happen? Because I'm pretty sure she hasn't got a thingy or anything. You know. A boyfriend. And all right she was hanging out with that crowd from Strange Hill again but she didn't seem to be actually <u>with</u> anybody. Definitely not that guy who looks a bit like Seb, anyway. He was too busy staring at Meera all night!

Mandy • AUGUST 22nd

Was going to do this when I got home last night but that was before Meera rang. By the time she'd finished gibbering and making various vowel sounds it was nearly 2 o'clock in the morning! And well, call me old-fashioned but I thought I ought to get a bit of sleep at some stage. You know, what with working in the morning and everything. Honestly though, that was some phone call! Anybody would think we hadn't just spent all evening with each other or something! Mind you, Meera made about as much sense on the phone as she had done earlier at Mashin' Impossible – i.e. very little. Boy, has she got the hots for this guy from Strange Hill or what? Which is great, but isn't she overlooking one teensy weensy thing? And, by teensy weensy, I actually mean glaringly obvious, by the way. Or am I the only one round here who thinks this bloke is more than a little like old DJ Substandard himself, Seb? Oh well, Meera's a big girl now. She knows what she's doing. At least I hope she does!

Meera • AUGUST 22nd

Is this a wind-up? Because if it is, it's not funny, it's just plain cruel! Posting a question like that on my web page. Getting me all hot and flustered. Who'd do a thing like that? Mandy certainly wouldn't. I mean, she likes a good laugh and everything but she knows me too well. Knows how insecure I am about my looks and stuff. No, it can't have been Mandy. So who was it then? Let's consider the evidence again, shall we? 'Dear Meera, I've got something to ask you. Did you ever get the feeling you were meant to be with someone? I did. Last night at Mashin' Impossible. Looking at you. Oops, have I said too much? The name's Dex by the way. Ciao4now. PS, I hear Screech 7 is supposed to be pretty good.' I mean, ohmygodohmygod!! It can't really be him! Can it? I don't even know if that's his name. And how does he know mine? I have so got to check this out! But how? Hang on. Steven's quite chummy with that geeky guy from Strange Hill, isn't he? Yeah, that's it! I'll get Steven to ask him!

Clare • AUGUST 23rd

So that's that then. We leave for Ibiza at the weekend! Wow! Abi's going completely mad packing already. Anybody would think we were emigrating, not just going for a week! Honestly, the amount of stuff she's taking! Me? I'm just going to bung a couple of things in a bag. I'll be fine as long as I've got loads of books to read, my toothbrush and a pair of sensible walking shoes. I still haven't got anyone to help look after Café Dot.Com while I'm away mind. I really must get that sorted. It needs to be someone I can trust. Someone hard working and responsible. Aye, and preferably health conscious too. Perhaps that's just too much to ask for though. Let's face it, most folk round here think that a balanced diet means a whopperburger and fries in each hand! I have to admit, the old beany stew's not been going too well lately. I don't know if it's got anything to do with that new rumour on the website or not. But, I mean, come on! Fruit And Mouth Disease? Oh well, I suppose I can always make it without the bananas. You know, just in case.

Steven • AUGUST 23rd

Been asked 2 do a bit of priv8 investig8ing 4 Meera. 1ts 2 no name of guy from Strange Hill. Found out from chatting online 2 David Davids 2day that guy's name = Dex. Weird because only yesterday David Davids 1ted 2 no what Meera's name was! PS, Have downloaded gr8 new track by Deathvomit! 1 of their slower 1s.

Almost ballad-like. Still kicks bottom tho. Called 'Even Fluffy Bunnies Have 2 Die Sometime'.

Seb • AUGUST 24th

So there's going to be an end of summer so-called 'Showcase Of Local' so-called 'Talent' is there, man? Er, like this affects me how basically? Precisely. It <u>doesn't</u>. Why? Because it's a sure fire guaranteed one way ticket to Loserville, Ohio, calling at Sad City and No Life Central only, that's why, man! For real. Yo! Listen up, right? Because the only way that I, The Real Slim Madely, purveyor of all that is impeccably cool, would even consider getting involved in something <u>that</u> desperate, would be if a) I was on an unstoppable mission to deliberately lose all credibility and respect with my fellow homies, or b) I was already dead, dude! And, as I was just saying in the chatroom, given that I'm neither, I'm going to have to give this so-called 'Showcase Of Local' so-called 'Talent', or BigBash.Com to give it its proper title, a Big.Miss, you know what I'm saying? Mos.Def!

Mandy • AUGUST 24th

Me and Meera have just been putting posters up for BigBash.Com all over the place <u>and</u> I've done a piece about it on the website. You know the more I think about it the more wicked I reckon this is going to be. Not that I'm any nearer knowing what I'm going to do, mind you. I still haven't got a clue. But the thing is, it's not just an opportunity for us lot to strut our stuff and do our party pieces. It's an opportunity for everybody! If the old codgers want to do a bit of synchronised bingo or whatever, then cool. If the Strange Hill mob want to do something, hey, that's cool too! The stage is quite literally their oyster, or whatever that saying is! People can do what they want basically. Hey, with any luck, the lovely Jason might even get up and show us what he can do! Wooooof!! Now there's a thought, ha ha!! Meera seemed a bit distracted by the way. Like her mind was on other things. She could hardly wait to get back to Café Dot.Com for some reason.

Meera • AUGUST 24th

Ohmygodohmygod, so his name is Dex after all!! Still doesn't necessarily mean the message was from him though. Someone could have faked it. But why? Well I'm going to stick my neck out and take a risk. I've just looked at my chart and well, what with Mercury rising at the moment, change is in the air. According to Psychic Sue, new and potentially exciting times lie just around the corner. But nothing's going to change unless I want it to change. Nothing's going to happen unless I'm prepared to make the first move. It's pretty clear then. I mean she might as well have said, 'Go for it, Meera!' But what will I say? I don't want to be too flirty, do I? I don't want to give the wrong impression. Not yet anyway! I know. Something about the film! Yeah, that's it! 'Dear Dex, you get the tickets, I'll get the popcorn.' That should do it! But I'm still not going to say anything to Mandy. Not yet. Just in case. Ohmygodohmygod!!

Craig • AUGUST 25th

You know what I really like about The Girl In The City Shirt? Apart from, you know, her eyes and looks and well, everything basically? The City shirt. Well, not so much the shirt itself although it is a perfectly nice one. No, it's more the fact that she wears it in the first place. Because, the thing is, you see so many flipping United shirts around these days, don't you? And most of these people have never been anywhere near Northchester in their lives. Just because United keep winning everything in sight! They're all just flipping fair weather supporters, that's what they are! Why don't they support their local team like I do? It makes me sick. But I'm clearly in a minority on this one. And so is she by the looks of things. I really admire her for that. Along with all the other stuff obviously. Now if only I can find out her name. Hang on. Steven's quite friendly with that nerdy guy from Strange Hill, isn't he? I could get Steven to ask him for me. Yeah that's it!

Steven • AUGUST 25th

More investig8ing. Am going 2 start charging 4 this. Could make small 4tune at this rate. Could af4d all CDs I 1t + still have enough left 4 Deathvomit T-shirt. (The 1 with picture of decomposing gerbil on it.) Me + David going 2 C them in Sheffingham. Can't wait. David getting band 2gether. Pity I can't play anything.

Clare • AUGUST 25th

We're going away with each other in three days' time, but Abi and I still haven't spoken about the other night. It's almost like we're both pretending it didn't happen or something. But it happened all right! Boy, did it happen! What I'm trying to figure out though, is why did it bother me so much? Why is it <u>still</u> bothering me? Because, I mean, it shouldn't, should it? It's a free world and all that. She can snog who she likes. Maybe it was just the shock of discovering that Abi isn't six any more! Yeah, that's it. At least I hope it is. Because another possibility would be that what really bothers me is the fact that it was Seb she was actually snogging. And why would that bother me? Because I'm jealous? Yeah right! As if! Anyway I'm still off men. I realise that might be a difficult concept for some people to get their heads round. Mentioning no names, but Mandy for instance. Mandy who can't even mention Jason without checking her hair and lippy first! Actually that's a point. I really must have a word with Mandy.

Mandy • AUGUST 26th

Flipping flipping flip flip!! I am <u>so</u> jealous of Clare and Abi going to Ibiza just like that, the lucky so and so's! I mean, there's me stuck in Molton all summer, slaving away in Safebury's for next to nothing and there's them jetting off to the Isle Of Totty for seven nights of heaven! The only consolation is that we won't have to put up with flipping beany stew for the next week! And I'll personally be making sure of that incidentally. Honestly, fancy Clare asking me of all people to help run Café Dot.Com while she's away! Is she mad? I have to say, it was actually quite funny, the way she asked. Yeah well, apparently she'd been hoping to get someone hard-working, responsible and health conscious to do it. But she couldn't find anyone, so she asked me instead! Ha ha!! Completely straight-faced she was too. I wasn't in the least bit offended though. I was too busy thinking of all the decent food we'll be able to eat now! In fact the sooner the pair of them go to flipping Ibiza the better as far as I'm concerned!

Seb • AUGUST 26th

It's a real shame for Abi, man. Going away so soon after sampling the delights of the Lurve Machine first hand the other night. Well, first tongue anyway. But, I mean, it's going to be a real wrench for her now, isn't it? Having to leave just when things were getting a bit tantalising and that. She'll be well devastated basically, you know what I'm saying? Oh well, that's life I suppose, man. As for me? Hey, what can I say? I'll get over it. In fact, I just have. Yo! Check this out, right? There was this totally foxy chick in the Dot.Com Centre today chilling with the Strange Hill posse. Not only that but she was sending out some serious vibes in my general direction. Vibes which basically said, 'Your place or mine, dude?' Mos def. So I like, immediately sent back these vibes which said 'Can't you see I'm busy, baby?' Just to let her know who calls the shots around here. Just to let her know she's dealing with The Sebmeister, you know what I'm saying? And, as a matter of fact, I <u>was</u> busy. Busy chatting in this kicking chatroom Steven's told me about. She'll be back though, man. It's only a matter of time.

Craig • AUGUST 26th

Davina! Her name's Davina! Wow! Sounds dead exotic, doesn't it? Sounds like she should be a dancer or something. Well, I've made my mind up. The next time I see her I'm going to come right out with it. No more dithering. I'm going to ask her out. Or am I? I mean, what's the worst possible thing that could happen? She could say no and I suffer a crushing blow to my confidence, followed by another long spell of self-doubt and introversion and, who knows, possibly years of therapy and psychoanalysis. But, I mean, apart from that, what's the worst thing that could happen? Oh god, I wish I knew what to do! I wish I knew how girls' minds worked. It says in *Men Are From Margate Women Are From Vauxhall* that all men have a female side and that we should get in touch with it more often. Well I've tried to get in touch with mine but it's never in! Maybe I should ask Meera again? She's a girl. She'll know what to do. No! I'm going to ask her out! Oh god, this indecision is driving me crazy! Or is it?

Meera • AUGUST 27th

Well that was fairly conclusive, I suppose. Not only is his name definitely Dex, but he definitely left that message. And at least there's no need to worry about whether to say anything to Mandy now, is there? Not since Mandy was there when it all happened. When Dex walked straight up to me in Café Dot.Com tonight and asked me if I wanted to go to see *Screech 7* with him tomorrow. And yes, I suppose I am being rather cool about this, aren't I? Hang on a minute. Aaaaa- aarrrggghhh!!!!!!! That's better!! Honestly though, you should have seen Mandy's face! It was an absolute picture. Her jaw just about hit the ground! Especially when I just said, yeah, why not? You know, dead casual. What made it even more pleasing was the fact that I know perfectly well Seb clocked the whole thing, out the corner of his eye, while he was in the chatroom or whatever it was he was doing. Of course he pretended not to, but then he would, wouldn't he? But hey, enough of ex-boyfriends in the file marked 'History'. Let's get our priorities right here. What will I wear tomorrow? Hmm, I can feel a text coming on!

PS, Who <u>was</u> that girl hanging out with the Strange Hill crowd? Honestly, talk about full of herself!

Seb • AUGUST 27th

Well, I don't know if that was meant for my benefit or not, man, but all I can say is that if it was, it backfired big-time, you know what I'm saying? For real. I mean, what does this guy want, a medal or something? Strutting around like he owns the place. Thinking he's it. Thinking everybody's looking at him, in his shades and his combats and his stupid hat and his 'ooh look at me I'm being really subversive and cutting-edge' Tweenytubbies T-shirt. Check this out, right? I was wearing one of those suckers at least two weeks ago! Yo! When it comes to being subversive and cutting edge, the guy's clearly a lightweight, man. Not even worth bothering about. Which is precisely why I wasn't bothered, dude. I'm still not bothered, even now. Not even a little bit, you know what I'm saying? I could tell Meera and Mandy weren't impressed either. I could tell they were just like, tolerating him basically. Big up Meera and Mandy for that by the way. Respect due.

Mandy • AUGUST 27th

Honestly, what is that girl like? That's the seventh text Meera's sent in the last half an hour, going on about what she's going to wear tomorrow! What can I say? I'm happy for her, I really am. She's my best mate and I love her to bits. So as long as she's happy, what's the problem? I'll tell you. It's just that, well, lust is blind sometimes, isn't it? Basically your mind can just turn to mush in the presence of top quality totty. Hey, I should know. Been there, done that, got the T-shirt, baby! How many times have I passed on all that getting to know you stuff and gone straight for the tonguenastics? Virtually every time! Oh, I don't know, I just don't want to see Meera get hurt that's all. Maybe this Dex guy's perfectly OK. There's just something about him though. I wish I knew what it was. Mind you at least me and Meera agree about one thing. Just who does that girl from Strange Hill think she is? And it's nothing to do with the fact that she's really gorgeous. Oh well, time to start planning Café Dot.Com's carefully balanced and nutritious menu for the next week, I suppose. I want to vary things so that we don't end up having exactly the same thing every day. So let's see. Chips the first day, French fries the second! Now that's what I call varied! Ha ha!!

That's it then! We're just waiting for the taxi to the airport. And then it's *adios* Molton! *Hola!* Ibiza! Well, for a week anyway. Aw, what a shame though, missing Mashin' Impossible tonight. Because, I mean, I really wanted to spend another Saturday evening watching Seb making a complete armpit of himself, waving his hands about in the air, talking utter gobbledegook in that ridiculously phoney accent and 'rocking the joint with his ill sounds and phat beats'. And if you believe that you'll believe anything! I am <u>so</u> looking forward to spending some time away from this place it's not true. Steven's been telling me about all the different ways I'll be able to keep in touch. There's really no excuse not to either, what with e-mails, chatrooms, message boards, text messaging and good old-fashioned telephones, too! They're even setting up a webcam at the Dot.Com Centre. So all I've got to do is find a nice wee Ibizan cybercafé somewhere *et voila*! Café Dot.Com in glorious technicolour! Not that I'm planning on doing that, mind you. This is supposed to be a break. And, anyway, the place is going to be in safe hands. Well, Mandy's anyway. Hmm, perhaps I ought to make a note of the website address anyway. Just to be on the safe side.

Steven • AUGUST 28th

Café Dot.Com all day 2day. Have never ea10 so many chips. Mandy says it's what Clare would have 1ted. That's good e-nuff 4 me. Will miss Clare but aim 2 respect her wishes. Hope she gets in touch soon. Was chatting online 2 David Davids. David wearing gr8 new Slipsnot T-shirt, by the way. Doesn't know what 2 call his band though. I suggested Mukus. David seemed 2 like it. Says it defin8ly rocks. Says I should start new website called Bandname.com. Not sure but think he was joking.

Craig • AUGUST 28th

What can I say? This has to be one of the best days of my life! Well, so far anyway. But I tell you, this one really is going to take some beating! Where do I start? At the beginning? Bor-ing! Nah, we'll start at the end. The bit that's only just happened. The bit where I got to walk Davina home from Mashin' Impossible! The bit where we stood on her front doorstep and looked at each other dead meaningfully! The bit where she . . . wait for it . . . leaned forward and tilted her head over to one side and opened her mouth slightly! And, OK yeah, the bit where the door suddenly opened and she introduced me to her dad! But by then it didn't really matter. I was already in heaven! Actually her dad was really cool about it. He just said hi and asked us if we'd had a nice time and went back inside again. Davina and I looked at each other like we didn't really know what to do. Then she gave me this quick peck on the cheek and said that she'd phone me! Even discovering that she does actually go to Strange Hill after all hasn't changed the way I feel. Who cares? Big deal! I've decided that love has no boundaries! I still can't quite believe it happened. I still keep expecting to wake up any minute now. Female side? Who needs a flipping female side? I've got Davina!!

Meera • AUGUST 28th

OK, so what's the catch? There has to be a catch! Doesn't there? Or perhaps the catch is that there isn't a catch! Because, I mean, talk about a perfect day! Talk about a dream date! Talk about top totty!! Ohmygodohmygod basically! Dex is so nice. Everything just went so brilliantly. I mean, he turned up for a start, which is always a plus in my books. He looked totally drop dead gorgeous too, which is a double plus in my books! He even insisted on paying for my ticket and popcorn, but in a strictly non-patronising and non-sexist way. There's something quite refreshing and old-fashioned about him actually. Because, I mean, the adverts were practically over before he tried to snog me for the first time and, according to Mandy, that's just unheard of. The film was absolute pants by the way, or at least the bits I actually saw were. But then you can't have everything, I suppose. We went to Mashin' Impossible afterwards. Me and Dex. Dex and me. Like a proper couple, in fact. And, boy, can he dance or what? Even with Esinem DJ-ing! We're talking SSOAS here! That's <u>Serious</u> Sex On A Stick!! I'm practically hyperventilating just thinking about it all now! What was it I recommended Confused Of Molton should use to relax? Lavender oil? I'd better give it a go. It's either that or I go and live in a convent!

Seb • AUGUST 28th

Yo! Diary! Check this out, right? Once upon a, you know, time, not so very long ago, I was totally cool with the Strange Hill Massive chillin' at the Dot.Com Centre. I was down with that, you know what I'm saying? Mos def. But listen up, man. Because that was then and this is like, totally now basically. This Dex guy is beginning to seriously get on my nerves. I mean, he still doesn't bother me. I don't find him a threat or anything. I just find him irritating, man. Seriously irritating. What was he trying to do tonight? Dancing in the middle of the floor like that with everybody stood round watching. That's if you can call it dancing, of course. I call it flailing around in a random fashion without any sense of style or rhythm whatsoever, you know what I'm saying? Unless, of course, he thought he was being terribly anarchic and cutting edge and generally out there. In which case he was sadly deluded, man, because it was none of those things. It was just plain embarrassing. Actually, I think he realised he'd blown it, because afterwards he just skulked off into the night and that was the last we saw of him. Meera left at the same time funnily enough. Coincidence? Had to be, dude. What else could it have been? Still no sign of the foxy chick, by the way. Hey, I can wait, man. I wonder what her name is anyway.

Mandy • AUGUST 29th

Flipping Safebury's! Who needs it eh? Well actually I do. How else am I expected to support my retail therapy habit? Seriously though, it's getting tougher and tougher, dragging myself out of bed first thing on a Sunday morning. Especially when it's the morning after Mashin' Impossible. My head's still throbbing from all that racket Seb was churning out. Call me old-fashioned, but I thought the whole idea was that the more you practise something the better you get! If it is, then no one told Seb! Oh, and so much for first impressions. Yeah well, I was talking to that girl from Strange Hill last night. The one me and Meera thought was dead full of herself. And, of course, she turned out to be really nice! I mean, she can't help being gorgeous, can she? Cow! Oh her name's Jade, by the way. Anyway, I wonder how Meera got on with Sexy Dexy. I'm dying to know. And what about Craig? I mean, do those two look like they're made for each other or what? And I don't just mean the City shirts either. I just think they look really good together. Actually, you should have seen Craig at work today. Floating around with this big stupid grin on his face, stacking shelves like it was the greatest job in the world. Which reminds me, I must buy another staff discounted case of Coke for Café Dot.Com. Supplies are running dangerously low. If I don't act quickly we'll be forced to do something we might later regret. Like drink apple juice! Yeah right. As if!

Craig • AUGUST 29th

Davina Davina
sweeter than Ribena
it was love when I first seen ya
my Davina.

Davina Davina
I howl like a hyena
when I think of you not Tina
my Davina.

Davina Davina
my devine Davina
you define devine Davina
my Davina.

Steven • AUGUST 30th

Just call me Steven Stevens Priv8 Investig8or! Got 2 find out name of foxy chick from Strange Hill. Just 1 problem. Have no idea what foxy chick means. Fox which looks like chicken = contradiction in terms 2 me. Will ask Seb. Am defin8ly going 2 start charging 4 this! Has happened 3 times now! Could af4d entire Mama Roach + Damp Bizkit back catalogue at this rate. PS, Have been asked by David Davids 2 watch next Mukus rehearsal. Cool.

Meera • AUGUST 30th

Well either {:¬) <>~{}~#`¬^)?! actually means something, or Mandy's finally lost it! Let me see now. Well, if you look at it sideways the first bit looks quite like someone wearing a beret smiling, I suppose. Maybe she wants me to go to France with her or something! But then the next bit looks like a fish! Oh, I don't know. I think I'll just give her a ring and see what she's on about. Maybe that's it? She just wants me to call her! No doubt to fill her in on the Dex situation. Why didn't she just say so in the first place? <u>And</u> I've got a new question on my web page. Hey, am I Ms Popular all of a sudden or what? Actually, it's quite funny. It just says 'Dear Meera, can you recommend anything for an extremely irritating cousin? Please help me. I'm desperate. Yours, Stressed of Ibiza'. Poor old Clare! Doesn't sound like she's having much of a holiday, does it? You know I never thought I'd ever say this, but I think I might actually be starting to miss her. In a weird kind of way, obviously. Having said that, I'm not missing the beany stew one teensy bit! Heck no! Now then. 'Dear Stressed, re your ICS, or Irritable Cousin Syndrome . . .'

Clare • AUGUST 30th

Well, I don't know whether Meera ever intends taking this agony aunt thing up professionally at some stage or not but, for the general public's sake, let's hope that she doesn't! Why not? Do you want a list? Honestly, she rattled on about everything under the sun <u>except</u> what I actually asked her about! Still, it was good to hear all the latest news. And, boy, there certainly seems to be plenty of it what with one thing and another! Meera and this Dex guy! Craig and Davina! I'm away a couple of days and what happens? Everybody starts copping off with each other like there's no tomorrow! I mean, what's going on? Has Molton Secondary suddenly been twinned with Strange Hill or something? You know, I never thought I'd ever say this, but I think I might actually be starting to miss that place. Not that I'm jealous or anything because I'm not. And besides, I'm still off men. Which is more than can be said for Abi, by the way. Honestly, what is that girl like? I tell you, there's not a bloke on this island who's safe as long as Snogzilla's around! And to think I still thought she was just a wee highland lassie. Yeah right. And I'm Britney Houston!!

Mandy • AUGUST 31st

Still haven't got a clue what I'm going to do for BigBash.Com. Mind you, neither has anybody else by the looks of things. The response so far to the posters and my thing on the website has been, let's say, minimal. Or to put it another way, totally pathetic. I can't believe that not one single person wants to get up on that stage and do their party piece and basically just show off for a few minutes. Honestly, what a bunch of lightweights! I don't know, maybe they just need a bit of incentive to shake off those inhibitions? Perhaps there should be a prize for the best turn? Yeah, like some personal one-to-one tonsil tennis coaching from yours truly for instance. Of course, I'd have to fix things so that a bloke won. But that could be arranged. And, at this rate, it might be the only way I'm ever going to get another decent snog round here! Honestly, talk about feeling like a complete gooseberry. Everyone's at it except me! OK, so maybe I'm exaggerating a bit, but when Craig's getting face to face on a regular basis and I'm not then you know for sure that the world's gone mad! At least, I presume he's getting face to face. It's been three days after all. That's practically a long term relationship isn't it? Well, for me it is anyway, ha ha!

Craig • AUGUST 31st

Davina just called! Actually called me! On the phone! I mean, how great is that? I tell you it's like something out of a book! Well, for me it is anyway. But it gets even better. Because she wants to see me again at the Dot.Com Centre tomorrow! I know, unreal, isn't it? I really feel like this is it now though. Like this is the start of something big. Like I've finally finished my warm up and it's time for me to join the rest of the human race. Something like that anyway. But what am I going to do till tomorrow? Mind you it's nearly bedtime now. When I wake up it'll already be tomorrow! But what if I can't sleep? My heart's pounding! My hands are all clammy! I need to relax. What was it Meera said I should do? Put what in the bath? Oh Davina, Davina! I'm finally going to do it! <u>We're</u> going to do it! I just know we are! It might not be tomorrow but who cares? We'll do it when the time is right for us. When we're ready to take our relationship that one stage further. And when we do? Boy, it's going to be some kiss!

Seb • AUGUST 31st

Hey, look I know I might have said that cybercafés were strictly for the nerds and like, one big geek magnet basically. And to a certain extent that might still be true. But I tell you what, man, chatrooms are seriously exempt from that somewhat sweeping generalisation. Check this, right, and remember where you heard it first when you're reading all about it in the Sunday supplements. Chatrooms totally rock! For real! Well, for me they do anyway. For me they totally float my boat, you know what I'm saying, man? See, the way I look at it is that they're a medium for spreading the word. Yo! The word according to The Sebmeister, lapsed Spokesdude of this parish. They're a means of imparting my insight and wisdom to those who might need it. And let's face it, man, that's pretty much everybody. Yeah, and not only that, but they're well wicked when it comes to finding out stuff you might not want others to find out about if you know what I mean. Like the identities of certain foxy chicks for instance. So big up Steven and David. Respect due. And big up Jade too. Who, by the way, could very easily be given access to all my areas if she plays her cards right, you know what I'm saying, dude? Mos def.

September

Steven • SEPTEMBER 1st

Went 2 C Mukus rehearse 2day. Sounded gr8. Wri10 loads of 2unes. No words tho. No singer either. David Davids says if 1 came along soon they might play @ BigBash.Com. Cool. Gr8 grub @ Café Dot.Com 2day. Burgers + 'finely sliced pot8oes deep fried in oil until golden brown + lovingly garnished with salt + ketchup'. Wouldn't tell Mandy but looked like chips 2 me. 1der how Clare is. Meera knows e-mail address. Will maybe contact l8er.

Meera • SEPTEMBER 1st

Hmm, that's interesting. Dex seems to think he knows Seb from somewhere, but can't quite think where. Says there's something vaguely familiar about him. Not that

Seb realised he was being scrutinised. He was way too busy staring at his PC to notice us. Honestly, they make an unlikely-looking threesome, Seb, Steven and Steven's mate, sat there tapping away all day. Oh well, each to their own and all that I suppose. Me and Dex just dropped by Café Dot.Com to see Mandy, by the way, and to have a quick burger and Coke. Jade was there too. She's dead friendly. Not at all like we thought she was. So anyway then Dex asked to have a look round the rest of the Dot.Com Centre. And well, one thing led to another and before we knew it we found ourselves alone in this really dark room. Well, you hardly need to be Psychic Sue or Kosmic Kate to predict what happened next! And very nice it was too. Yeah, until the lights suddenly went on and we realised we were in the middle of a photography workshop! That's why it was so dark! They were all developing their own prints! Meanwhile Dex and I were stood there giving a public demonstration of synchronised tonguenastics! Dex was incredible though. He didn't bat an eyelid. He just looked around, dead coolly, and said, 'Oh sorry, isn't this Contemporary Dance? We must be in the wrong room!' Honestly, I didn't know whether to die of embarrassment or wet myself laughing!

Hurrah! At least one person's going to be doing something at BigBash.Com. Who? Craig of course! Not that he knows it yet, mind you. But he is, even if I have to flipping well make him. I mean, how long have I been banging on about how funny he is? The guy's a natural born comedian and the sooner he and everybody else realises it the better. God, you should have heard him at work today, going on about Davina and how she's so great because she actually wears a City shirt and not a United one! What, like that's some kind of big deal? Personally speaking I take all kinds of qualities into consideration when it comes to assessing a prospective hunk. Snogability factor? Absolutely. Passing resemblance to the blond one from Westfield? Yeah, great, why not? Colour of shirt? Who cares? Unless of course it's really <u>really</u> horrendous! Talking of which, what <u>was</u> Clare wearing today?! I don't know, maybe it was just the quality of the webcam picture or something, but that multicoloured top thing she'd got on was unbelievable! Mind you, judging by the tanned beach god whose lap Clare was sat on at the time it was obviously a top totty magnet! Hmm, wonder where I can get one. Ha ha!!

Hey, what can I say? That I tripped and fell on his lap? That I sat down without checking if the seat was free or not first? That he suddenly appeared out of thin air, just as I was about to sit down? Nah, still doesn't sound terribly convincing, does it? How about I just thought och to heck with being off men, if you can't beat 'em join 'em? You know, when in Rome do as the Romans do, and all that? Except that we're not in Rome, we're in Ibiza. But not for much longer. Another few days and we'll be back in Molton. I'll go back to being off men then! And, I mean, I don't want to be a killjoy, now do I? Abi's been having such a great time. It seemed a shame not to chum her along to that club and keep her company. And there <u>are</u> only so many museums and galleries you can go to, aren't there? And there <u>is</u> only so much time you can spend with your parents. And Miguel <u>is</u> so completely and utterly drop-dead gorgeous! And to think, if the coin had come down the other way up we'd have probably been cooped up in some smelly wee boat right now, pootling along some canal in the middle of nowhere at about five kilometres per week! Oh well, there's always next year I suppose. Aye, or failing that, the year after!

Wow! Me? Do some stand up comedy at BigBash.Com? I'd not thought of that. Actually, I'm really not sure if I've got the bottle. Let's face it, it's not exactly me, is it? Getting up on stage in front of loads of people and just, well, talking and stuff? I don't know how those guys do it. Why put myself through something that nerve-wracking? Because, I mean, I've already done what I set out to do. I've used my irresistible sense of humour to win Davina over. Mission accomplished and all that. By the way, we still haven't, you know, done it. We still haven't kissed. But Davina did give me another peck on the cheek when I walked her back home again last night. Boy, can she peck on the cheek or what? It was practically X-rated! I'm going all funny just thinking about it. It's definitely only a matter of time before . . . well, before we take things to another level and kiss each other properly. At the same time. With tongues and everything. Apart from that though it's all going brilliantly. Well actually, there is one thing we don't quite see eye to eye on. Davina thinks that I might take football just a little bit <u>too</u> seriously. And I . . . how can I put this? . . . don't basically! But it's not a huge problem as far as I'm concerned. I mean, at least she wears the right colour of shirt! It's not like she's one of those fair weather supporters or anything, is it? Now that <u>would</u> be a problem!

Seb • SEPTEMBER 2nd

Yo! Come in Jade, your time is like, up basically. It's time for you and me to stop playing these silly mind games and get better acquainted. It's time to let nature take its true course. It's time to get seriously horizontal, foxy lady, you know what I'm saying? So if you want to jump aboard The Sebmobile and take a trip to the Planet of Lurve then cool, I'll gladly be your pilot. I'll take you places you've never been, baby. Mos def. Just ask Meera. 100% satisfaction guaranteed or your money back! But hey, if you don't want to, then equally cool. As I was saying online just now to my homies, Steven and David, there's plenty of other chicks in the queue who'll happily log on to Seb.com. All I have to do is say the word and they'll come running, baby. If you know what's good for you though and you're generally up for it, you know where you can find me. Yo! Behind the decks at Mashin' Impossible, cutting up banging beats and kicking tunes, keeping it phat and phunky, but above all, keeping it real! The choice is yours, foxy lady. So what's it going to be? To Seb, or not to Seb? That is like, the question.

Steven • SEPTEMBER 2nd

Been in priv8 chatroom with David + Seb 4 most of day. Good job it <u>was</u> priv8 2. Some of stuff Seb was coming out with was like l8 night documentary on Channel 6. Un4tun8ly didn't understand 2 much. Will maybe log on 2 Seb.com 2 answer queries. Gr8 burgers + 'pot8oes *à la* Mand' in Café Dot.Com 2day, by the way. Remarkably cheap 2.

Meera • SEPTEMBER 2nd

Ohmygodohmygod! <u>What</u> is Seb like? Going on to Steven and his mate about what a love machine he is! OK, so strictly speaking they were in a private chatroom. I wasn't meant to see it. But I couldn't help it. Honest! Steven left his PC for a few minutes to get something to eat and I just happened to be passing. I glanced over, you know, like you do, and the very first thing I happened to read was something about taking a trip to the Planet of Lurve on The Sebmobile! I mean, come on! What was I supposed to do? <u>Not</u> read the rest or something? Some of the stuff he was coming out with was unbelievable. Actually, that's not true. <u>All</u> of the stuff he was coming out with was unbelievable! I tell you, Seb's wasting his time DJ-ing. He should be writing science fiction! As for the bit about me, well, what can I say? The only time Seb ever took <u>me</u> to a place I'd never been was the day we went to Sheffingham. And even then <u>I</u> paid for the bus fares! Ohmygodohmygod, I have <u>so</u> got to text Mandy about this! We have so got to warn Jade!

Mandy • SEPTEMBER 3rd

This is priceless! Absolutely priceless! Seb is <u>such</u> a plonker it's not true! Seb the plonker from the planet Plonk! Meera's dead right. We have to save Jade before it's too late. Actually, Jade seems more than capable of saving herself from what I've seen, but if my little scheme goes to plan we could have a right laugh anyway! And talking about schemes, I'm going to have to think of something pretty damn quick before Clare gets back tomorrow. Why? I've only gone and blown a whole month of Café Dot.Com's budget in five days, haven't I?! Yeah I know, oops! Clare's going to hit the roof! But I mean that amount of burgers, chips and Coke doesn't come cheap. And I probably have been under-pricing stuff a bit. But what the heck? It's been fun. And at least it hasn't felt like a flipping health farm round here for the past week! So what am I going to do? I've got to restock the store cupboard for next to nothing and quick! But how? Well I could always dip into my hard-earned retail therapy reserves and pay for stuff myself. Yeah right. Like that's going to happen! Alternatively I could get Steven to surf around a bit and see what he comes up with online. Let's face it, he owes me one. He's been putting away enough burgers lately! Yeah, that's it. This sounds like a job for . . . Superhighwayman!!

Clare • SEPTEMBER 3rd

Was that really a burger and fries I saw Craig eating on the webcam tonight? Are they deliberately trying to wind me up or something? 'Ooh, let's kid on to Clare that we're all stuffing our faces with junk food whilst she's away! Tee hee!' Because if they are! . . . if they are! . . . well, so what basically? Who cares? I certainly don't. Not any more, anyway. Not since the lovely Miguel and Juan kindly volunteered to be my and Abi's personal guides for the rest of the holiday! Personal guides? Phwoar, if I'd known Miguel could snog like that he could have had the job for the whole week! Plus he's dead romantic and keeps giving me all these flowers and chocolates and stuff. It's fantastic! Forget all that museums and galleries garbage! Talking about romance, Craig certainly seems to have fallen head over heels for this Davina girl, doesn't he? He's a sweet guy,

Craig. Dead funny too. I mean, fancy going to all that bother getting in touch just so he could ask me to bring some lavender oil back from the airport with me!

Steven • SEPTEMBER 4th

Have wr10 sum words 4 Mukus song. All about the way I am + way I feel inside + how sometimes I get frustr8ed + inarticul8 + can't rel8 v. well 2 other people + the world about me + stuff. Song is called 'Everything Sucks'. Seb says it's v. catchy. David Davids says it rocks. Even 1ts me 2 try singing it! 1st reaction = Aaaaarggggghhhh!!!! 2nd reaction = Cool! Am going 2 rehearse 2nite. 1ce I've finished browsing 4 cheap same day online food delivery site like Mandy asked me 2. Will maybe try searching 4 Cheapsamedayonline fooddelivery.com. That should do it.

Craig • SEPTEMBER 4th

I really wish Mandy wouldn't keep banging on about flipping BigBash.Com every time she sees me because I'm not going to do it. No way. I can think of far easier ways of being publicly humiliated than that. Like walking down the street with the Incredible Pregnant Woman, or Mum as she's more commonly known. And, anyway, it's only a few days away. I wouldn't have the faintest idea what to do. It's not like I've got a ready made routine rehearsed or anything. I guess I'd just get up there and tell a few jokes. But it's not going to happen. End of story. Mashin' Impossible tonight, by the way. It's getting really popular, actually. You know for all the slaggings he gets old Esinem must be doing something right I suppose, otherwise people wouldn't be coming back week after week. OK, so some of the stuff he plays is still totally unlistenable, but it doesn't matter because there's a really good buzz about the place. Anyway, the last thing I'm bothered about is the music if you get my drift. Seb could play FClub Heaven and Britney flipping Houston all night long for all I care as long as the light of my life is there! Oh Davina, Davina, sweeter than Ribena, it was love when I first seen ya, my Davina . . .

Seb • SEPTEMBER 4th

Yo! Diary! Check this out, right? It would appear that the High Priestess of Foxiness herself, Jade, has finally come to her senses, you know what I'm saying? Big up Jade basically. Maximum respect due, leaving that message on the message board and stating in no uncertain terms her desire for an immediate one way, and strictly non-returnable, ticket to Seboslovakia.

Funnily enough though, man, there were other messages for me as well. From other chicks. Chicks I don't even know. But all equally foxy. All with the same intentions. Intentions involving me and them. Yo! And we're not talking line dancing, man, you know what I'm saying? For real. Which is well weird basically. Because I didn't really mean that stuff I was saying the other . . . I mean I was only . . . well, anyway I've got all these messages, dude. And now I don't know what to do, dude. All of a sudden it's raining chicks. But there's only so much of me to go round. Hey, what can I say? I'll find a way, man. After all, I'd hate to disappoint the laydeez. Word. Seb out.

Meera • SEPTEMBER 5th

Poor Seb! I'm actually starting to feel a bit rotten about it now. It seemed like such a laugh last night too. But now I'm not so sure. OK, so he'd been acting like a complete slimeball, bragging about his alleged exploits and what a 'lurve machine' he was and all that. But still, was that really a good enough reason for us to take the mickey out of him like that? In front of everybody at Mashin' Impossible? I don't know. God, it <u>was</u> funny though, me, Mandy and Jade all turning up at the same time in those identical sparkly outfits and wigs and throwing ourselves at him like that! Seb just didn't know what to do! His eyes were practically popping out of his head! Mind you, I don't blame him. What <u>must</u> we have looked like? Honestly, I've never worn anything quite that tight before in my life. I've still got the stretch marks to prove it! I'm amazed he didn't recognise us though, but then I suppose it was pretty dark in there. Oh god, and then when Dex strolled in right on cue and we immediately ran over and draped ourselves around <u>him</u> and gyrated about? I thought I was going to wet myself, I really did! And the look on Seb's face when we suddenly whipped off our wigs and collapsed in hysterics! Talk about gobsmacked!

Mandy • SEPTEMBER 5th

Well, Meera might feel sorry for Seb but <u>I</u> don't. He was bang out of order going on about his love life like that, if you ask me. Just because I don't actually <u>have</u> a love life at the moment. What was he trying to do? Make me jealous or something? And then when he started talking about Meera like that? Well, that was it. Drastic measures were called for. I've said it before but I'll say it again. Mess with my best friend and you mess with me, mateypants! I don't know. Some people just never learn, do they? I have to say though, we were absolutely brilliant the three of us. Not forgetting Sexy Dexy, of course. He did his bit as well. Yeah, and according to Meera he did his bit later on as well! Wooooof!! Lucky cow! Anyway, it's given me an idea for BigBash.Com. If the others are up for it, of course. Five days to rehearse? No problem! Actually, I've just announced on the website that there's going to be a mystery prize for the best turn on Friday. It certainly is a mystery too, because I haven't got a clue what it'll be! Ha ha!! Maybe I'll leave that to Jason. Let him decide. PS, Clare's back, looking fit and well and with this big stupid grin all over her face. She doesn't seem to have noticed any difference with Café Dot.Com. Phew! Think we got away with it! Nice one, Steven.

Steven • **SEPTEMBER 6th**

Mandy v. gr8ful 2 me 4 helping her out of po10tially sticky sit2ation. But like I told Mandy, don't thank me thank Cheapsamedayonlinefooddelivery.com. Mandy says I have defin8 talent 4 internet + stuff + that I should use it. Actually, have thought of online chips delivery. Big demand 4 chips in Molton. Well from me + David Davids, anyway! David thinks my singing is cool by the way + that 'Everything Sucks' still defin8ly rocks. Think Craig can rel8 to words of 'Everything

117

Sucks' right now. V. un4tun8 about him + Davina.

Craig • SEPTEMBER 6th

How could she? How could she do this to me? I really thought we'd got a good thing going. I really thought we were right for each other. I thought we were meant for each other. OK, so I wasn't sure about the whole Strange Hill thing to begin with. But I dealt with it. I learnt to accept it. Like I say, love has no boundaries. But this? This was much, much worse! This was worse than having a permanently pregnant mother! This was in a different league altogether! And it had to happen in front of everybody else, didn't it? Like it wasn't bad enough already! I tell you, I'm a shadow of the man I was this time less than two days ago. I still can't quite believe it happened. I mean, how could she? Knowing how I feel. Knowing what it would do to me. How could she turn up at Mashin' Impossible wearing a flipping United shirt? I didn't say anything. I couldn't say anything. I didn't need to say anything. I just turned and walked away. Oh Davina, Davina, Davina. Oh well. It was nice while it lasted, I suppose.

Clare • SEPTEMBER 6th

Oh, what the heck? If they want to eat burger and chips every day then fine! Aye, as long as they're <u>vege</u>burgers, of course! I mean let's not go <u>too</u> mad here! I might have lightened up a bit lately, but I still have my principles. I'm not sure how much of the aforementioned lightening up can be put down to the therapeutic effect of Miguel and his amazing heat-seeking tongue, mind you. Whatever. Hey, and talking of principles, poor old Craig eh? Just when things were starting to go well for him, too. Practically tripping over his face today he was. He just looks totally crushed by this whole Davina thing. As for Seb. I thought he was decidedly subdued, sat there at his PC next to Steven and his mate from Strange Hill. Mind you, he livened up all right when Meera and Dex came over. I'd love to know what they were talking about. Whatever it was certainly seemed to get Seb going and a wee bit more like his usual self. It's all quite intriguing, actually. I've obviously got some catching up to do. Never mind a week, it feels like I've been away for six months! And, by the way, what <u>does</u> Dex think he looks like with that blond cropped hair of his? He's as bad as Seb! Oh well, better be off. Abi and I are supposed to be working on a little something for BigBash.Com right now. We tried it on holiday as a matter of fact and found that we were pretty good at it. I won't spoil the surprise, but it's kind of a speciality in Ibiza. So you see, Miguel wasn't the only local talent I picked up while I was out there!

Seb • SEPTEMBER 6th

Dex borrow my decks? He's having a laugh, man. I tell you, there's more chance of me and Jade living happily ever after in perfect domestic bliss with 2.4 dudelets and a conservatory than that happening, you know what I'm saying? For real. I mean the idea of him ever getting his amateur hands on my trusty turntables is a total non-starter. As for the idea of this guy actually DJ-ing at BigBash.Com? Well he's obviously got a sense of humour. Well, I mean, he must have, mustn't he, what with that new so-called haircut and so-called name of his. What is it again? Deminex? Yeah right, man, dream on. Why Meera can't just see straight through this guy is like, a complete mystery to me basically. He's an impostor. A total fraud. He's about as street as my mum. Not that I'm dissing my mum, you know what I'm saying? Big up my mum! I mean Marjorie. Anyway the point is, man, this Dex dude couldn't keep it real if his life depended on it. Yo! And purely for the purposes of research, I'm prepared to prove it. Look, I know I said there was no way on earth I'd ever get up and do anything at BigBash.Com, but well, it would appear that I no longer have any choice in the matter. Let battle commence, dude. Mos def.

Meera • SEPTEMBER 7th

Honestly, how juvenile can you get? Compared to Seb, Dex is just so mature. Mind you, so is anybody compared to Seb. My three-year-old niece is mature compared to Seb! He just can't handle it, can he? Can't bear the thought of anyone muscling in on his territory. Can't bear the thought of not being *numero uno*. So he has to resort to posting personal insults and playground taunts on the message board. Didn't have the guts to do it face to face. Didn't even sign his name. Didn't have to. It was so obviously Seb. 'Mos def' this and 'for real' that. I mean, you don't exactly need to be a detective to figure it out, do you? Maaaaan! As for all that stuff about stupid names and haircuts? He-llo! Earth to Seb! We have a serious pot-calling-the-kettle-black situation here! At least I know that there's no danger of Dex being tempted to reply. Dex is way above that kind of thing. I mean, that would be just so tacky, wouldn't it? Oh, anyway, I should just forget about it, I suppose. It's really not that important. What's important right now is me and Dex. Mind you, even Captain Testosterone is going to have to go on the back burner for a couple of days whilst me, Mand and Jade practise our thing for BigBash.Com. Honestly, that is going to be <u>such</u> a laugh!

Steven • SEPTEMBER 7th

Seb came 2 C Mukus rehearse 2day. Started jamming along on decks. Sounded gr8. Dead heavy + rocky but with defin8 hip hop feel 2 it. Seb said it was 'fat and banging'. Have no idea what that means. Think it's good though. Craig bit better 2day. All fired up about sumthing. 1der what? Clare v. upbeat 2 considering what she saw on webcam. Clare so nice. Much 2 good 4 him anyway.

Clare • SEPTEMBER 7th

Well, you learn something every day, don't you? And the thing I've learnt today? Men really <u>are</u> the same the whole world over! Honestly, what a lowlife! Look, I wasn't kidding myself that Miguel was the great love of my life or anything. I mean, it was just a wee holiday fling after all. But to sit there, knowing perfectly well that I could see him on the webcam and still let some shameless floozy virtually use him as a sunbed? Aye, and then to discover from Abi that Miguel had tried it on with <u>her</u> every time my back had been turned? Put it this way. I'm definitely off men again. Well, actually, I'll maybe ask Jason a wee favour first. But <u>then</u> I'll definitely be off men again. For good this time! Anyway, summer's nearly over. We'll be back at school before we know it, up to our eyes in A Levels and studying. There'll be no time for extra curricular activities, if you know what I mean! Besides, Abi's not going to be around to lead me astray if I feel myself starting to waver. Actually, I'm really going to miss her when she goes back, my innocent wee cousin. Innocent? Aye right. And Westfield write all their own songs!

Craig • SEPTEMBER 8th

OK, so four days ago there was no way I was ever going to do any stand-up at BigBash.Com. Then again, four days ago I thought I was hopelessly in love and in a fully fledged, committed relationship. Well, strictly speaking, still not quite fully fledged. But almost fledged. Never will be fledged now by the looks of things. Anyway, I wasn't going to do it then, but I am now. So what? Call it therapy, call it channelling all my pent-up anger and energy into something completely different in order to try and take away the pain, or just call it plain flipping crazy. Who cares why I'm doing it? What am I? A flipping psychiatrist or something? I'm doing it and that's all there is to it! And relax. Phew, that's better. Well, now I've got that little lot off my chest I suppose I ought to carry on working on my routine.

Mandy • SEPTEMBER 8th

So much for old SuperDex being all mature and above that kind of thing then. Meera was so cross when she looked at the website she couldn't speak. Literally! She had to text me instead! Told me to look on the message board and see if I thought she'd been a little hasty and maybe misinterpreted things slightly. But let's face it, there's only so many ways you can interpret, 'Deminex thinks! Esinem stinks!' and, 'Deminex rocks! Esinem sucks!' isn't there? Well, one to be precise. As a matter of fact it sounds like a bit of a challenge, if you ask me. Sounds like the old gauntlet being thrown down, or whatever it was they used to throw down in the olden days. You know what? I've got a funny feeling my funny feeling about Dex might be about to come true. I reckon there's going to be a showdown on Friday. I reckon there's going to be a big bash in more ways than one! I reckon there's going to be a battle of the bottle blondes! Ooh, watch this space eh? Keep it locked on Mand FM! Ha ha!!

Seb • SEPTEMBER 9th

Just want to make one thing clear, man. Despite appearances to the contrary, this is <u>not</u>, I repeat not a climb down. No doubt. I've simply changed my mind and decided to let the guy use my decks after all, you know what I'm saying? Even if he has got a stupid name. And a stupid haircut. It had nothing to do with him finding out . . . well, it had nothing to do with anything basically, man. I just thought, hey why not? If he wants to have a go, then great. If he wants to pit his lamentable DJ-ing so-called skills against those of a true sonic master, then that's up to him. If he wants to suffer public humiliation and degradation on a previously unimaginable scale, then who am I to stop him basically? Yo! I've said it many times before, man, but it is a free world. At least it was the last time I looked, you know what I'm saying? Mos def. So roll on Friday as far as I'm concerned, baby. Let's kick this thing off. For real. In the words of the Godfather of Soul himself, Mr James Brown, bring it on, man, bring it on. Yo! Or in the words of another true musical genius and innovator, my name is . . . my name is . . . my name is . . . Slim Madely!!

Well hey, what do you know? Dex has redeemed himself by finally remembering where he knows Seb from. Apparently . . . ohmygodohmygod this is <u>so</u> brilliant . . . apparently, they used to go to the same . . . wait for it . . . pony club together!! Can you believe that? They weren't both members of the same inner city street gang. They didn't used to hang round with the same bunch of 'homies' in one of Molton's more notorious 'hoods'. They were in the same <u>pony club</u>! OK, so it was a long time ago. But even so, can you imagine? Seb, aka DJ Sebsonic, aka Spokesdude For A Generation, aka Esinem decked out in jodhpurs, tweed jacket and hard hat? It's true though! I've seen the photo! Dex was going through some old albums the other day and bingo! There they were! Grinning away, eight years old, proudly holding up rosettes, but unmistakably Seb and Dex! Talk about hysterical! Hysterical and very useful as things have turned out! Yeah well, I thought I'd mention it to Seb and see if it might somehow persuade him to let Dex use his turntables after all tomorrow night. And amazingly enough it worked! Of course, Seb tried to bluff it out at first, claiming that he'd only done it for a couple of weeks and that even then he'd insisted on 'keeping it real' by wearing his hat back to front! But when I suddenly had the idea of putting the photo up on the website so that everybody could see it, he changed his mind straight away! Funny that eh? God, I wish I could tell Mandy! But I can't. I've got to stick to my side of the bargain. For now anyway!

Clare • SEPTEMBER 9th

Wow! Jason really is a pretty good actor! He's wasting his time running the Dot.Com Centre. He should be on the telly, or on the stage or something! Let's face it, the guy's got the looks. Not that I'm interested, of course, what with being off men again and everything. But, I mean, the way he just happened to casually saunter over and ask me how much longer I was going to keep him waiting. And I just happened to tell him to wait his turn like everyone else. And I just happened to be talking online to Miguel at the time. And the webcam just happened to be on. It was just so perfect and natural. Like it hadn't been set up and rehearsed at all. Like there really was some kind of spark between us. Which would be ridiculous, obviously. Because I mean there isn't any kind of spark. And because I'm off men. And even if I wasn't, Jason's old enough to be . . . to be . . . well he's old enough to be my boyfriend, actually. Theoretically, of course. But, I mean, he's probably only twenty or something. That's not a huge age difference, is it? Theoretically, of course. Good grief, get a grip, Clare! It's not going to happen! I only did it to give Miguel a taste of his own medicine. I just wish it hadn't seemed quite so right, that's all.

Steven • SEPTEMBER 10th

Things 2 do b4 BigBash.Com 2nite:

1. Shout a lot in order 2 lose voice.
2. Go near sum1 with laryngitis + breathe deeply.
3. Clean bathroom + accidentally swallow bleach.
4. Search web 4 Handycures4reallybadstagefright.com.
5. Relax (ask Craig 4 whatever it is he uses).
6. Make another list.
7. Repeat steps 1 – 6 @ regular intervals throughout day.
8. Emigr8.

Mandy • SEPTEMBER 10th

Just got back from BigBash.Com. You want the lowdown on the showdown? Well, the truth is, there wasn't really a showdown after all. The big stand-off between Seb and Dex just didn't happen. I know. Bor-ing. It was almost like there was this strange kind of unspoken truce between the pair of them. Almost like some weird mutual respect thing. So I don't know what's been going on there. If Meera knows anything then she's keeping pretty tight-lipped about it. We did our thing, by the way, Meera, Jade and me. Knocked 'em dead we did, miming and dancing and generally shaking our collective (and personally speaking) ample booties! And though I say it myself, Destiny's Chicks was a pretty damn good name! Mind you, I'm still not too sure what the significance of the riding gear was. Meera wouldn't say. Unless of course the jodhpurs were designed to make my booty look even <u>more</u> ample. In which case, result! Ha ha!! Craig was just brilliant, by the way. I knew he could do it if he stopped trying to reel off jokes and was just himself. He was so funny. Why Jason gave Clare and Abi the mystery prize though, and not Craig, I have no idea. I wouldn't be a bit surprised if it turned out to be a fix. And, anyway, weren't they supposed to be doing something dead cultural and Ibizan? Call me old-fashioned but that was karaoke! Talking of Ibiza, guess where I'm saving up to go? Ibiza! Since when? Since I copped another eyeful of the lovely Miguel on the webcam just now and he copped an eyeful of me! One word. Woooooooof!!

Clare • SEPTEMBER 10th

Well, I have to say, I do actually feel a bit of a fraud. I mean, there's no way Abi and I should have got the mystery prize tonight. For a start, Mandy, Meera and Jade were great. And, if anything, Craig was even better. All that stuff about snogging and his mum being pregnant! What a laugh! My sides are still aching. As for Seb and Steven's wee 'collaboration'? What can I say? Is Steven Stevens a total rock god or what? He might not say a great deal but, boy, can he sing? Honestly, what a voice! Goodness knows how he gets it to sound all raspy like that. He must gargle gravel every morning or something! Couldn't understand a word he was on about, mind you, but with hindsight I think that was probably a good thing. Anyway, what I'm trying to say is that in all honesty I don't think we really deserved the prize. And I was fully intending giving it to someone else. Honest. Aye, until I found out what the prize actually was. Dinner at a restaurant of your choice with the lovely Jason! Hey, what's a girl supposed to do? Hmm, pity Abi's going to be tagging along as well, but then you can't have everything, can you?

Steven • SEPTEMBER 11th

Am in complete st8 of shock. Can hardly speak. Last nite just incredible. Nerves seemed 2 vanish the moment we started. Felt so good. Felt so right. Seb gr8. David + other guys gr8 2. Everything gr8! Mukus rocked! Can't wait till next gig. Feel strangely MT now. Like there's void inside me that needs filling. Will get some more chips. That should do the job. PS, Am so happy 4 Craig. PPS, Thank you Molton and goodnite!!!

Craig • **SEPTEMBER 11th**

What happened last night? Can someone please fill me in because, to be honest, the whole thing's a bit of a blur. I remember walking out on stage and starting my routine. I remember making a complete hash of the first joke and then just kind of drying up. I stood there for a few seconds, wondering what the heck I should do. Then what? Well, I think I must have just started talking. Just, you know, chatting. About stuff in general. I wasn't trying to be particularly hilarious or anything. It just all came pouring out. But they really seemed to like it. It felt really good. And then the next thing I knew, it was all over and people were coming up to me and telling me how much they'd enjoyed it! And then? Well, and then Davina came up to me and told me how much she'd enjoyed it! And I remember standing there and looking at her and thinking you idiot, Craig! You stupid, great flipping idiot! Letting a ridiculous thing like the colour of a football shirt overrule your heart! Because it was obvious to me in that moment that me and Davina really did have a good thing going. We might still have. You know, if Davina gives me another chance and everything. And it looks like she might. We're going to Mashin' Impossible with each other tonight! Yes! Yes!! Yes!!!

Seb • SEPTEMBER 11th

Yo! Diary! Check this out, right? Was I awesome last night or what? I mean did the joint rock, or did the joint rock? Was I in the house, or was I in the house? Want to big up my man, Steven, and my man, David Davids, and the rest of my backing band too, by the way, you know what I'm saying? Also want to big up Dex. Well I mean, obviously I don't want to big him up too much. But credit where credit is due, dude. The dude did OK, dude. You know? DJ-ing? For real. I mean, not amazingly or anything, but he was OK. Kind of. For a total beginner. And yeah, he seems like an OK kind of a guy. But that's as far as it goes, man. I don't want anyone running away with the idea that we have a potential happily-ever-after situation on our hands, because we don't. Me and him aren't suddenly going to become inseparable or anything, but there's no reason why we can't coexist peacefully and harmoniously, you know what I'm saying? And talking about harmonies, man, I've decided to generously extend the offer to Jade to make sweet, sweet music with The Sebmeister anytime she wants basically. Because she was looking well foxy last night. You know, despite the riding gear? Or maybe <u>because</u> of the riding gear, man. Hey, whatever. All I know is the chick still clearly wants my body big-time. Yo! And if she plays her cards right she can still have it, dude! Mos def. Seb out.

Meera • SEPTEMBER 11th

Well it looks like that's that then. Come in please summer, your time is up. School starts Monday. Then before you know it, it'll be Christmas. Then Easter. Then summer again, then Christmas and so on and so on. Some people reckon time is a mystery, but it seems pretty straightforward to me! Ohmygodohmygod, though, Upper Sixth! I still can't quite believe it! Dex and I are going to have to make a bit more of an effort to see each other from now on, I suppose. But love, as Craig says, knows no boundaries. If it means getting a bus to the other side of town for a decent snog, well then that's the way it's got to be. Not that we're actually in love or anything. But it's going OK. And anyway the Dot.Com Centre's going to be staying open. There'll still be Mashin' Impossible every week. Who knows, maybe Dex will even get to DJ sometime! Yeah I know, sounds horribly familiar, doesn't it? Oh well. Seb's been very nice to me and Dex since our little chat a couple of days ago, by the way. I don't know. What is that boy like? I have to say though, him and Steven were actually pretty half decent last night at BigBash.Com. I must remember to tell Steven next time I see him. That's if I can get close enough to speak. That lavender oil's pretty powerful stuff! Got to go. Just got a text from Mandy. Haven't got a clue what it means, mind you. I suppose I'd better phone her and find out.

Also available from Piccadilly Press, by
JONATHAN MERES

Another term at Molton
Secondary, and life goes on as
normal. Well, that is if you
call a potentially disastrous
Ofsted inspection, an
outbreak of graffiti, a
rampaging serial snogger and
the antics of the Rat
Liberation Front 'normal', of
course.

Meanwhile . . .

• Will Meera have to have
her mobile surgically
removed?

• Will **Mandy** ever find fame
and fortune? Or will she just settle for a decent bloke?

• Will anything ever happen to **Craig** that isn't completely
rubbish?

• Will **Steven Stevens** ever manage to string more than two
words together?

• Will **Clare** stop her crusading when the new golden boy
Troy starts to show some interest?

• And will **Seb** finally admit that Dennis and Marjorie might
just be his real parents after all?

*"Another year at Molton Secondary sees the usual chaos
and hilarity with all the favourite characters in another
effervescent diary novel."* Books magazine on YO! DIARY! 2

'Joseph, are you in there?
It's me, your mother.'

Damn, I thought it might
be that Jennifer Lopez again;
she usually calls round about
this time for a quick snog.

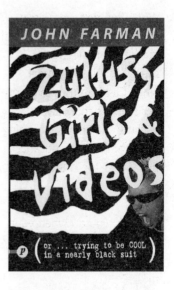

Zulus I always think my
life's a bit like living in that
old film *Zulu* – you know,
the one where Michael
Caine (me) and a bunch of
rather hot British soldiers
(Rover) are holding this garrison fort in Africa somewhere
against thousands of ever-so-cross natives (my family).

Girls This is really sad. One minute my head's full of the
gorgeous, sexy Jade, and whether I might stand a chance
with her after all, and the next, I'm thinking of dear sweet
Lucy. Jade–Lucy, Lucy–Jade, I just can't get my brain straight.

Videos I'm a complete cinema junkie – a filmoholic – a
movie maniac – a video voyeur, you name it. I don't know
why, but all I ever think about is films (oh yes – and girls).

"Lively, witty text by a diverting writer." Publishing News

When Ben first sees Cassie
Sinclair he thinks she's special.
But he has no idea how
special she is. They meet
when Cassie refuses to go on
her school's coach trip
because she knows it is going
to crash. Ben is sceptical at
first – until the coach really
does crash.

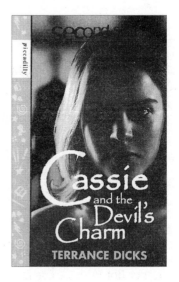

What do you do when your
new best mate can read
minds and see into the
future?

Exept try to look out for her. And that's when the trouble
starts.

And when Cassie's lawyer mum becomes involved in a deal
with a very powerful financial entrepreneur the trouble starts
big-time. Ben and Cassie know there's something dangerous
about this man and she's determined to figure it out . . .

The first in an exciting new series by *'the master of the genre'*,
Terrance Dicks.

*"A compelling book by one of the most reliable of children's
authors."* Publishing News, Starred Choice

Sunday 8.00 p.m.
Walking home, I said, "I don't think he's that keen on her. What sort of kiss do you think it was? Was there actual lip contact? Or was it lip to cheek, or lip to corner of mouth?"

"I think it was lip to corner of mouth, but maybe it was lip to cheek?"

"It wasn't **full-frontal snogging** though, was it?"

"No."

"I think she went for full-frontal and he converted it into lip to corner of mouth . . ."

Saturday 6.58 p.m.
Lindsay was wearing a thong! I don't understand **thongs** – what is the point of them? They just go up your bum, as far as I can tell!

Wednesday 10.30 p.m.
Mrs Next Door complained that **Angus** has been frightening their poodle again. He stalks it. I explained, "Well, he's a Scottish wildcat, that's what they do. They stalk their prey. I have tried to train him but he ate his lead."

I flopped on the beanbag next to her. I felt happy. Iz and me. Me and Iz talking about stuff and Iz predicting my future.

'What does it say, Madam Rose?'

'Oh interesting,' Iz murmured. 'Very interesting. The card that crosses you is the Wheel of Fortune. It signifies a new chapter. A turning point.'

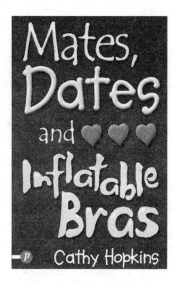

But a turning point is exactly what Lucy does NOT want. Everything is changing around her, and suddenly she is required to make all sorts of decisions.

• Everyone else knows who and what they want to be except her.
• Izzie has become friends with the glamorous Nesta and Lucy isn't certain she likes this new threesome.
• Nesta and Izzie look sixteen, but Lucy, at fourteen, can easily pass for a twelve-year-old.

But then the day Lucy sees the most wonderful boy crossing the street, things do start to change – in all areas of her life . . .

Georgie's life is falling apart. Her mum is in a psychiatric hospital and her dad just isn't coping. No one has any idea what's going on in Georgie's head. And what's going on inside Georgie's head worries her. A lot. Her teachers say she isn't trying herd enough and her friends say she is dead weird. Georgie is pretty sure she's slowly going mad like her mum.

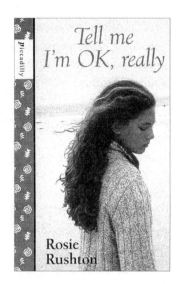

Then, just when she thinks she has lost it, Georgie meets Flavia Mott, a woman who at first seems even dottier than Georgie's mum. And suddenly Georgie finds herself opening up for the first time in years. But is it already too late for Georgie? Will she ever be OK again?

From the highly acclaimed author of:
The Leehampton Quartet
The Girls series
The Best Friends trilogy

If you would like more information about
books available from Piccadilly Press and how
to order them, please contact us at:

Piccadilly Press Ltd.
5 Castle Road
London
NW1 8PR

Tel: 020 7267 4492
Fax: 020 7267 4493

Feel free to visit our website at
www.piccadillypress.co.uk